PEN PARANORMAL

By

ANNIE NICHOLAS

Vanguard Elite, book 4

Penny of the Paranormal

Table Contents

Chapter One
Chapter Two
Chapter Three
Chapter Four
Chapter Five
Chapter Six
Chapter Seven
Chapter Eight
Chapter Nine
Chapter Ten
Chapter Eleven
Chapter Twelve
Chapter Thirteen
Chapter Fourteen
More Books by Annie!
About Annie

Note to Readers

Every time I return to the Vanguard world, it's like taking a trip down memory lane. I've never been the type of person who fits in with the popular crowd. I marched to the beat of my own drum, even now as an author. So why wouldn't I love writing about the outcasts of the wolf shifter packs. Sometimes a woman just wants to root for the underdogs.

To receive updates on future releases, contests, and events join my mailing list.

Penny of the Paranormal

Chapter One

Penny couldn't sleep. Her growling stomach kept her awake. The candle on her nightstand was still lit but burned low. Though it was day outside, the setting winter sun hovered on the horizon and didn't give her much light. On fleet feet, she hurried to the only bathroom on the girl's floor to take a shower before it grew dark and a line formed.

They were a mixed-gendered group. The third floor housed the males and the second floor the females. Each floor had eight bedrooms—double occupancy rooms for the girls and quadruple for some of the boys. Since the boot camp had started, at least a third of the pack had been sent home, so the numbers had changed. Males weren't allowed in the female area and vice-versa.

The candle flickered with Penny's sudden run, but it didn't extinguish. The manor didn't have electricity except in the kitchen to keep the fridge cold.

The empty fridge.

Ignoring her hunger pains was growing harder with each day. The boot camp's taskmaster was a vampire who was old as dirt. He controlled the lack of electricity, their nighttime schedule, and the food. If they didn't like it, then they could go home.

But some of them didn't have homes to return to. Worse, for others like her, home meant an abusive pack. A little hunger and cold wasn't too much to pay for her freedom.

Penny's breath misted the air. No power meant no heat or hot water. In a household filled with sensitive shifter noses, she didn't dare skip washing. Even if it meant risking frostbite.

She stripped out of her layered clothes, folded them, and set the pile

Penny of the Paranormal

within reach of the shower so she could dress quickly afterwards. A thick layer of snow covered the boot camp's grounds. This was normal for upstate New York, but she was from South Carolina. They didn't get this much snow.

No matter what any human thought, the cold bothered *this* shifter. Her wolf form was covered in fur, not her woman form. She jumped under the ice cold stream of water and bit back a yelp. After weeks of cold showers, she would think she'd be used to the shock.

At light speed, she washed, dressed, braided her long, wet hair, then made her way to the kitchen to start the evening fire. Since Pallas, their taskmaster, was a vampire, the pack kept his nocturnal hours. She paused at the entrance, breath in throat.

Alistair Montgomery Carrington the Third roamed along the counters, searching the empty cupboards. He wore only his ass-hugging jeans, which were a work of art in denim. Hard muscles rippled under his sun-kissed skin as he stalked the kitchen.

She sighed. This was how a woman should start her night.

He spun at the sound and pinned her with his green glare. Stubble covered the sharp angles of his handsome face, making him appear more rugged and masculine than when he first arrived at the manor in his suit and Porsche. The same dirty blond hair that grew on his head appeared in a small spot on his chest, tempting a girl to curl her fingers in the patch.

"Where is all the food?" he asked.

She blinked. "What?"

"The cupboards and fridge are all empty."

She should be used to seeing Alistair half-naked. She'd nursed him back to health after Julia had shot him in the leg. He had deserved it, but Penny had never been able to deny help to any creature in need. Not even the arrogant ones.

"It's good to see you on your feet." She'd been wondering if he'd ever get off the bed Pallas had allowed him to occupy during his convalescence.

He scowled. "I've been healed for over a week. You know it."

"Yet you stayed in bed until now." She suspected it was the wound to his ego that had kept him hidden in his room, more than the one to his strong leg. She almost sighed again at the memory of his tight ass as she'd dressed his wound, but she needed to stop mooning over things that could never be and start the fire. "There's been no food for days." She set her candle on the hearth and gathered kindling. No lighters or matches were allowed per silly vampire dictate. They had nothing to cook, but they did have tea, and the warmth would be very welcome.

"I don't understand. You've been bringing me food until last night." He sat next to her, so close the heat radiating from his body caressed hers. It was as if he was made of flames, making it so tempting to curl against him.

"I gave you what I hid, but that's all gone."

He had needed the food more than she to finish healing his emotional wounds. With shifters, it always came down to food. It cured all their aliments. She'd suffered hunger before hence her compulsion to always have a hidden store of food. It wasn't easy to ignore the pangs. When shifters got ravenous, they tended to go feral. The boot camp pack already didn't like Alistair because what had transpired between him and Julia. If he went feral, they'd kill him, and that would be a shame.

"Did the boot camp run out of money? Because I can buy groceries. Shifters shouldn't be hungry."

They hadn't seen this other side of him like she had. The generous hunter who worried about shifters who were not even his pack. He'd been misled by his alpha. It was easy to do when a shifter wanted to please their more dominant pack mates.

As an omega, Penny knew all too well how simple it was to fall down that hole. During all those times she'd cared for his wound alone in his room—since no one would share one with him—he'd treated her kindly. She couldn't say that about most male hunters. Many shifters saw omegas as easy targets, and they were. That didn't mean those hunters should prey upon their own kind.

Fire bloomed under her hands as she brought it to life with the candle. "Pass me those logs."

Alistair's spine went rigid, and the scent of surprise surrounded him.

She watched him carefully from the corner of her eye. "Please." She held out her hand. Though he'd been kind, that didn't mean he wouldn't turn on her. She'd learned that lesson as well. Life as a shifter wasn't easy. Not like how the media portrayed it on television. Sometimes she felt surrounded by pumped up jerks just looking for a reason to fight.

He handed her a log then rose in one fluid motion. "You should be careful. Ordering a hunter could be harmful if you were in another pack as an omega."

"Good thing I belong to this one." She knew him. Better than he knew himself, she bet. He was right though, which was why she'd come to the boot camp. Omegas weren't treated well even when their daddy was the alpha. Her old pack was male dominated, unlike this one, where Clare was just as alpha as her mate, Ian. Her new alphas did things differently. They left her alone to do as she pleased. Freedom of will was a new concept. A cherished flower she guarded. She smiled up at Alistair. "It's kind of you to offer to provide us with food."

"A pack of starving wolves is dangerous. I can't believe Ian and Clare would allow this kind of abuse—"

"But we were ordered not to buy more food," she interrupted him. Something else she wouldn't have dared a few weeks ago. "This is a school, which Pallas runs. Ian and Clare lead the pack but have no control over the school. So no groceries."

The flames took, and she added more logs until a fire roared.

"You're good."

Penny of the Paranormal

She twisted around. "I've been building the fire every day since I arrived."

Alistair loomed over her, the light from the hearth the only illumination since the sun had finally set. He was a creature of shadow and flickering light. "No, I meant putting *out* my fire." He helped her stand.

Regret making her heart weigh a thousand pounds. She hadn't wanted to extinguish his fire. It was a defensive habit to keep the hunters around her calm. For once in her life, she wanted to make a man burn and instead she'd doused him.

"I never would have eaten your food if I'd known you were hungry." He wrinkled his brow. "You've been so kind to me." He tilted his head. "I hear your stomach growling."

She pressed her hands against her belly. "Nothing to be done about it now."

The familiar stomp of boots descended the back stairs. Pallas crossed the kitchen. "Outside with everyone else, Penny."

Most people's blood froze when they met her taskmaster. She knew better. Evil wore many faces, but it didn't wear his. Not since she'd met him, anyway.

Alistair dragged his gaze from Penny, wishing they could have a few more minutes alone. She was rarely by herself, especially when with him. He didn't think she was aware of how her pack quietly protected their only omega. There was always a shadow following her or standing outside his room when she came to check on him.

Instinct drove wolf shifters harder than any supernaturals, and since he'd been at the boot camp, he could hear his clearer than ever.

Storming after Pallas, he caught him at the entrance to the basement where the vampire made his home. "Why are you starving the pack?" Alistair gripped Pallas's arm and tried to spin him around. His fingers slipped free. He

Penny of the Paranormal

might as well have tried to move the manor with one hand.

The vampire paused before facing him. "Don't you mean, why am I starving you?"

"I can leave to eat whenever I want."

His gaze focused on Alistair and leaned forward. "So why don't you?" Pallas wasn't a typical vampire who liked to play seduction games. Bald with pointed ears and teeth similar to a shifter in beast form, he seemed more monster than man.

Alistair had no answer to Pallas's question, nothing he was ready to admit to, anyway. Except he wasn't ready to return to his pack with his tail between his legs. That was the only thing he knew for sure. He'd been sent to retrieve Julia, his betrothed, whom he hadn't loved, and had been beaten fairly, in front of the whole damn pack. "Starved wolves are dangerous. Do you want them attacking the humans in town?"

Before Alistair could blink, Pallas had him by the throat, his feet dangling as the vampire lifted him like a pup.

Annie Nicholas

Strong fingers prevented Alistair from breathing.

"Little wolf, do you presume to tell me how to run things? How many warriors have you trained in your short life?" Pallas set Alistair down, then shoved him back against a wall. "You seem well enough to travel. Don't overstay your welcome and tempt me to snack on you." Pallas strolled out the front door, the cold winter wind blowing a trail of snow over the threshold.

"Making friends again, I see." Ian, the pack's alpha, stood at the foot of the staircase.

Alistair rubbed his sore throat. "I've fought vampires. Never one that strong."

"Pallas is in a class of his own." Ian pointed to Alistair's neck. "He used that move on me the first time we met. It'll be sore to swallow for a day or so. Depending on how fast you heal."

"There's no food to swallow."

"About that." Ian pulled Alistair into the pack's living room and handed him a sweater. "You've shared our food, we've healed your wound, and given you

Penny of the Paranormal

shelter longer than you needed all because Penny begged us to."

"Julia shot me!" She was his ex-fiancé, and she'd used the gun on him in front of the whole damn pack like a rabid dog.

"You deserved it." The alpha crossed his arms, leveling a glare. It was good one for such a young alpha. He must practice in a mirror.

Everyone was of the opinion that Alistair had deserved to be shot. Obviously, he didn't agree. Well, maybe he agreed a little bit. But seriously, he'd done what any hot-blooded shifter male would have. He'd claimed what had been promised him from birth. Shifters fought challenges all the time over less. He didn't understand why they were so bent out of shape. The only thing he could see was that Darrell and Julia were their friends and he was the outcast.

"We don't have time for this." Ian's scowl deepened. "You owe us."

Alistair opened his mouth to protest.

"More." The alpha poked him in the chest. "You owe Penny."

That silenced any of Alistair's complaints. For once, they agreed, but he wouldn't admit that out loud.

Alistair pulled the thick sweater over his head. It was cold, and he'd been shirtless for Penny's benefit. She was always the first one up to make the fire and cook breakfast. He had hoped to cook her one this morning before the pack rose. Plan thwarted. He loved how her eyes lit up whenever she caught him shirtless.

"I'm listening." If she needed him, then he would help. She'd gone beyond the call of duty in caring for his well-being.

Ian took Alistair by the shoulders, tossed him a winter jacket, and guided him out the front door. "Pallas is planning another one of his missions. I don't know the details, but they've been escalating. My gut says this will be bad. Especially since he's starving us."

Alistair gritted his teeth at the implications. Ian was right. The stories of past training exercises had reached Alistair's ears. The vampire had a

Penny of the Paranormal

twisted sense of teaching. One shifter had died, and there had been a few close calls. "What about Penny?" He didn't know how she'd survived this long. It spoke of an iron core of strength, which he had glimpsed this morning when she'd asked him to do things without the usual omega meekness.

"We've looked out for her, especially Blain, but he's gone now. Clare and I have the whole pack to care for. That leaves Darrell and Julia. I'd like an extra pair of eyes watching my only omega."

A growl rolled in his chest. "She's not yours." It was out of his mouth before he knew it. Shifters weren't good liars, so he didn't bother to try. They tended to wear their emotions out in the open. He and his wolf nature were in sync, so this caught him by surprise.

"Everyone in my pack belongs to me." Ian pushed Alistair ahead onto the front porch of the old manor.

Pallas faced the pack, using the porch as a stage. "Nice of you to finally join us, alpha. I was just explaining that the boot camp is splitting into three teams."

The vampire returned his attention to the crowd gathered in the calf-high snow. "These teams will be led by Clare, Julia, and Penny. Ladies, we're doing a schoolyard pick. Clare, as alpha female, first pick is yours."

CHAPTER TWO

Penny startled at the sound of her name. "What did he say?" she asked no one in particular. Her heart pounded out of rhythm. Had he just assigned her a leadership role?

No, no, no.

Clare and Julia moved to one side of the snowy lawn, gesturing for her to follow.

She glanced around to be sure they really meant her. Darrell pushed her forward gently and she stumbled over her own feet. She twisted around.

A crowd of faces stared back and she fought the urge to hide.

Darrell gave her a wink, but she could see the worry behind it. Not just him. Everyone seemed on edge. The last mission had been rough and, not long ago, Pallas had vanished for a couple days. That couldn't be a good thing.

Her stomach rolled, not with hunger this time, but with nausea. Standing next to Clare, Penny could smell the stress coming off her in waves. It was hunger. That explained everything. Right? The pack looked worn, their eyes too bright, their muscles too tense. They needed soothing and calm.

They needed food.

She noted Ian and Alistair on the porch whispering frantically. What was Alistair doing with the alpha? They could barely be in the same room together without fighting. Both wore matching scowls as they stared daggers at Pallas's back.

The vampire ignored them. He paced the porch, moonlight sliding around him as if afraid to touch his flesh. The dark followed him like a shadow. "Start your picks."

Clare didn't hesitate in calling Ian's name, nor did Julia in picking Darrell. It made sense. They were mated couples.

She, on the other hand, had no one.

Anxious faces turned her way. No one wanted to be the last one chosen.

Penny of the Paranormal

She knew this firsthand being the meekest of her old pack. Human children were taught to play nice. Shifters couldn't afford that. They were taught at a young age to strive to be the strongest, the fastest, the most popular. Some wolves, though, weren't born with that instinct and were called omegas.

Well, that was the nicest name they called her kind. She'd heard much worse.

Most shifters weren't hunters of Ian, Clare, or Alistair's level. Otherwise they'd all be knocking each other's heads together. The core of their society lay with hunters like Julia and Darrell. Strong wolves happy to follow their alphas. These were the people who stared at Penny with expectations to lead them to victory.

She made her first pick.

Ian and Alistair exchanged confused glances.

Biting her bottom lip, she searched the crowd for inspiration and made her second choice. This wasn't easy. How did her alphas make decisions like this every day? Had she hurt anyone's feelings by not picking them first? She eyed her choices. Were they mad that she had picked them? She understood why Pallas had chosen Clare and Julia.

Clare was an alpha wolf one-hundred percent and Julia was training as a possible second to Clare. Why her? Omegas weren't leaders. She turned to her group with a watery smile. "We'll be fine."

Please don't die.

"I have planted three flags on the top of Mount Killmore." Pallas paced the porch, hands clasped behind his back.

Penny gave Clare a slow blink. "Where?"

The alpha female shushed her.

"Your mission is to retrieve your team's flag and return here." He paused with a sharp, pointed grin on his face. "No maps, no compasses, and with only the clothes on your back."

Oh God. Her stomach and heart exchanged places.

"You can't be serious," Clare shouted. "We'll die."

Penny of the Paranormal

Others joined in her protest.

"Enough!" Pallas's voice carried over the pack's combined complaints. They went silent. Experience had taught them not to piss off their taskmaster. He was fierce and merciless when he felt slighted. "If you were human, yes, most of you would die. Are you human?" He went silent. And waited. "I can't hear you."

They shuffled their feet, glancing at each other. "No," some called out.

Penny leaned toward Clare. "You have to find someone to take my place as leader."

Her alpha female shook her head. "He specifically chose you." She leveled her glare. "Don't you dare give it to someone else either. Pallas will find out and God knows what he'll do to you."

Penny swallowed with a throat gone dry. "Okay." Nobody on her team would want to be a leader anyway. She'd chosen them because they were the ones most likely to be left last.

A construction worker, a nurse, a chef, a florist, and a student. None of them major hunter material. All of them had been kind and thoughtful. She hadn't done them any favors by picking them first. She'd most likely killed them.

"Of course you're not human," continued Pallas. "You're wolves. Born of the wild, hunters of prey, trackers, survivors. All this modern tech shit has blinded you. In times gone by, all a wolf shifter needed was his pack."

Nick, the florist, slipped her hand in his and squeezed. "We've got your back, Penny."

Her heart swelled three times its size.

"If you're cold, you have fur and body heat. If you're hungry, hunt for food. Use your nose to track." Pallas glowered. "Stop your whining and go."

She noticed Alistair and Ian conspiring behind the vampire. What were they up to? She'd just patched Alistair back together—she didn't want him doing anything stupid. Pallas wouldn't tolerate any interference from an outsider.

People who pissed off the vampire tended to disappear. Her mind wandered to the hunters that had set the manor on fire. She hadn't regretted their vanishing act, though people in town said they'd moved away out of fear. She didn't believe it.

"Wait!" Ian raised his hand.

Alistair eyed him. What was he up to? He wanted to help Penny. The little omega would surely die on this mission, but what could he do? The vampire had made it clear he wouldn't change his mind.

Of all the crazy things he'd heard Pallas do, putting an omega in charge of a team was the craziest. Omegas were lovers, healers, caretakers. Alistair didn't know Penny's teammates but at a glance they didn't impress him with their competence.

"What is it, Ian?" Pallas seemed ready to bite someone.

"The teams are uneven. Penny is short one."

"She'll have to make due." The vampire turned away.

Ian gave Alistair a meaningful glare.

He sighed and gazed across the lawn where his eyes locked with Penny's. She shook her head, telling him not to do anything stupid. She didn't want his help?

Fuck. Shit. Fuck. Damn.

The sting in his chest was unfamiliar. It almost made him nauseated. What if he didn't volunteer and she died? All sorts of gruesome images played in his head of Penny freezing to death or getting lost never to be found. This wasn't a game. No matter what the vampire said, shifters could still die in the wilderness without proper training. Had Pallas provided them with it?

"I will join her team." He stepped forward.

"What?" The darkness around Pallas grew so dense Alistair could feel it pull on him like gravity. "You're not even part of the boot camp."

Alistair shrugged. "I don't hear any of the other teams objecting. Like the alpha said, it's only fair to have even teams." It took effort to keep his stance relaxed and voice calm when all he

Penny of the Paranormal

wanted to do was throw Penny over his shoulder and take her home to safety. In his pack, every nuance was watched and pounced on yet this moment seemed like the most important in his life. A turning point of sorts. If Pallas rejected his offer, then it was time for him to pack his bags and return to Texas, tail between his legs.

If the vampire accepted? His heart raced. He would be facing quite a challenge out in the wilderness in the winter with a team of—he eyed Penny's choices—less than standard hunters. It was a chance to prove himself.

What had she been thinking when she'd picked those wolves?

Two females and three males. None of who he recognized or seemed remarkably strong. He scratched his chin. He didn't exactly have a death wish.

Of all things, Penny appeared very unhappy at his volunteering. Perhaps she wanted to fail. With him on her team, that would make her task more difficult.

Pallas looked right through him. If he didn't know better, he would have guessed the vampire was trying to read his thoughts or something. But Alistair's mind was a steal trap.

"You have nothing to lose if you fail." The vampire circled him. "They all do." He pointed to the boot camp pack.

"I don't have anything to gain if I win, either."

"How do I know you'll make a genuine effort to help them?" The vampire's eyebrow rose, his grin chilling Alistair's soul. "A wager, then?"

Ian's face lit up. "Yes."

"No." Alistair shook his head. The vampire had nothing he wanted.

"Yes," the alpha insisted. "The car."

"No!" Pallas crossed his arms, yet behind him, the pack leaned forward as one.

"Yes." Alistair held out his hand for Pallas to shake. The vampire owned a sleek, black sports car that had been just delivered from the garage after the pack had been forced to bury it. "Scared my team will win?" He didn't care about the vehicle—he could buy ten of them if he wanted—but he needed Pallas to let him protect Penny.

The vampire eyed Penny's choices like he had. "Fine, but if they quit, you remain at the boot camp for a year and work for me." He gripped his hand, cracking Alistair's knuckles in the process.

Alistair swallowed the lump in his throat. The alpha was hopping with excitement. All Alistair really had to do was keep his team from quitting or dying. Piece of cake. His gaze locked with Penny's again and he shook the vampire's hand. "Deal."

Chapter Three

Part of Penny was excited to have Alistair on her team. She hadn't chosen her teammates for strength, like the other leaders. She'd picked them for their good character. If she'd known this would be a survival game, she might have picked differently.

Her gaze traveled over the faces of her group and her chest swelled with pride. No, she would still have picked them. Everyone had hidden talents and these five had something better. They had heart.

She just hoped Alistair could see this. He'd just bet a year of his life on them. No matter what happened they wouldn't quit. She almost snorted out loud at the idea that they might actually win. She would be satisfied with completing the mission without anyone getting injured—or worse—lost.

Penny of the Paranormal

The handsome shifter joined her team on the snowy lawn, his wild blond hair flying in the cold wind. He rubbed his hands together, not in anticipation, but because it was cold. "So who's who? You start." He nodded to Parker.

The thin and wry shifter jumped. "Parker, sir." The others followed suit, stating their first names—Nick, Amy, Vicki, Bobby Jo. She noted how Alistair paid close attention, repeating each name as if committing it to memory.

"I'm Alistair if you didn't know." He stuck his hands under his armpits.

She rolled her eyes. Like they didn't know who he was and hadn't witnessed the huge drama between him and Julia and Darrell. Penny tamped down a surge of jealousy. She understood why Julia had chosen Darrell over Alistair and she was glad for it. A complex shifter like Alistair deserved someone with patience and understanding. She just wished, for once, that someone would fight for her instead of expecting her to meekly accept their affection. They were always so surprised when she rejected them too.

The jerks. Like she should swoon and lift her skirts because they paid some attention to her.

Her father said that her behavior wasn't very omega-like. Too bad. He sent her here because he thought she was confused. That there was a hunter lurking in her heart. There wasn't. Being here made it even clearer that she wasn't like the others. She was weird and she was okay with it. Now, she needed to find a person who could love her differences.

The only people who treated her like she was normal were on this team. Excluding Alistair. He still treated her as if she had no free will. Though, he never tried to get into her pants. That actually stung a little.

The other teams were huddled together as if making plans. She signaled for everyone to gather close. "We need to find Mount Killmore and return. No food, no water, in the snow with only what we got." She tried for a confident smile but her bottom lip quivered. She held out her hand. "Here's to not dying."

Penny of the Paranormal

They left her hanging. No one placing their hand on top of hers.

Alistair rubbed the back of his neck, clearly trying not to laugh. He touched her hand and electric tingles ran over her skin. "Here's to not dying."

The others followed, someone gave a nervous laugh. "To not dying," they repeated quietly.

That was the worst pep talk ever. She cleared her throat. "So anyone know where Mount Killmore is?" That seemed like a good place to start. Who named these mountains? Seriously.

"It's northeast of here."

Alistair frowned in the direction Bobby Jo pointed. He took him by the shoulders and re-aimed his arm. "That's northeast."

Penny's stomach dropped. They were *not* going to die. As leader, she made this a silent command. She watched the other two teams depart in different directions. "We could just follow one of the teams before the moon sets and we can't see anything." Maybe they knew something her team didn't.

Pallas had taught them to use maps and compasses. She could find her way anywhere with these two tools, but without them she was pretty useless. She wasn't like Blain, who could track scents that barely existed. None of her teammates were.

"If I was one of the other teams, I'd start traveling in the wrong direction, waiting for someone to follow me then lose them." Alistair gave her an apologetic grimace.

"You think they'd do that to us?" The teams disappeared from her view into the woods.

"In a heartbeat," Parker added.

"Oh." She was so used to working as a pack. It was difficult for her to be competitive. Genetically, she lacked the shifter trait. "What should we do?" She wasn't the sort of person to lead blindly. Heck, she wasn't the sort of person to lead.

"You're in charge, Penny." Alistair was pacing around them, more than ready to go. The muscles in his jaw popped with the strain of his clenched teeth. Yet he didn't say anything else. Pallas had put her in charge. Sometimes, she came close to hating that vampire.

"Well, I'm not like the others. We take the direct route. Northeast it is." If someone wanted to follow, Penny was fine with it. She marched toward the forest.

"Why would anyone follow us?" She overheard Amy whisper to Vicki. They laughed quietly.

She didn't share their humor. She didn't care if they won, but she didn't want to be the pack joke either.

Penny glanced over her shoulder. "Chances are the others don't know where they are going either." There was truth behind her words, but she knew Ian, Clare, Julia, and Darrell well enough. They probably had well thought out plans by now. Where she was flying by the seat of her pants.

Her words seemed to give her team more speed in their steps. Alistair strode next to her, eyes scanning the trees.

Annie Nicholas

They didn't know where their destination lay yet Alistair's team strolled into the forest, blindly following Penny in the dark.

He watched for danger. Their group made so much noise that danger could have tracked them from a distance. There wasn't much that could threaten shifters, but he'd heard Ian's story about being shot by humans. Alistair had just recovered from such a wound and didn't care to repeat the mistake. It stung.

He checked over his shoulder every once in a while. His team followed in single file a little distance behind him and Penny. He didn't want to lose anyone. The wind was picking up and the temperature was dropping. Penny's teeth chattered so bad, he feared she would chip a tooth.

"Come here." He wrapped his arm around her shoulders, pulling her close to share body warmth.

She stiffened at his touch. "What are you doing?"

"Just trying to share warmth." She had nothing to fear. He'd never hurt her.

Penny of the Paranormal

He'd never hurt any female. An image of his mother cowering in the kitchen corner after his father had arrived home flashed through his mind. "Don't fret."

His mom had left them not long after.

"I'm not fretting. You surprised me." She leaned into him but there was still an aura of wariness around her. "I usually don't let strangers touch me."

Alistair blinked. Should he remove his arm from her shoulders? She could have shrugged him off anytime. Instead, he shared his warmth and soaked in her presence. Penny set him off balance internally. He knew how most shifters would act and react to him, but not her. "We're not exactly strangers."

"We aren't friends either."

Yet he noticed she still remained under his arm of her own free will. Pleasure curled in his stomach like a happy cat. "So am I your type?" He grinned, trying to misguide how important her answer was to him.

Sadness touched her eyes. "Yes, but it doesn't matter." Her shoulders finally relaxed and sighed. "Are we still heading northeast?"

He jerked his gaze from hers and scanned the area. "I don't know."

"What do you mean? You seemed to know at the manor."

"Sure, at the manor, I knew northeast because I've been there for days and seen where the sun sets. We've been walking these woods for hours. I haven't a clue where we are, let alone what direction."

Her shoulders deflated. "I'm the worst leader ever. We're already lost."

"I think that's the whole point of this exercise." Alistair lifted her chin. Her eyes were such a pure blue they reminded him of the sky on a clear summer's day. "Pallas wants us lost and stumbling in the woods. He wants us to survive."

"And the flags?"

"Bonus points. All he really wants is for no one to quit or die. He didn't say you'd fail without the flag." He could see her thinking.

"A loop hole?"

Penny of the Paranormal

"Exactly. My father's a lawyer. He's taught me to watch for these type of things." The asshole had some uses.

"I doubt Pallas will see it that way and he makes the rules. I'm not taking any chances of being sent home. We're going for the flags."

"I didn't say we shouldn't try for the flags. Nothing would make me happier than to see Ian's face when we beat him to the top, but it's not a priority. Staying alive and safe is."

"Well said." She stopped so suddenly he tripped over a hidden branch under the snow to follow suit.

"What are we doing?" Alistair rose back to his feet and wiped the snow off his knees.

She waited for the others to huddle around them. "First things first, Alistair was kind enough to remind me that this isn't a race and that stumbling in the dark, freezing our asses off can lead to unneeded injuries." She scanned the surrounding area. "Anyone object to this being our first campsite?"

Alistair scratched his head. Once again, Penny took a right when he expected her to make a left.

While the others milled around the wooded area, he did a quick security check. They had crossed a fast-flowing stream that hadn't frozen over so they had water. Check. It wasn't so deep that he worried about flooding. Check. He bent close to the ground, sniffing for territorial markings of the forest's natural predators. After circling the area, he found nothing. The trees helped shield them from the wind. This was as good a campsite as they were going to find tonight.

Nobody objected, including him.

"There's no reason to keep Pallas's night schedule." Penny yawned. "We'll move faster and surer in the day so let's make a camp and get some sleep. Maybe in the morning we can figure out if we're heading in the right direction."

He kicked a few stones clear of the snow. "The ground is frozen. We'll clear some of the snow away so it doesn't melt with our body heat and make us wet. Parker, don't you build houses for a living?"

"Uh, sure." The male shuffled his feet in the snow.

"Can you make us some kind of shelter? Nothing fancy."

Penny set her hand on Alistair's arm. "Can we speak in private?"

A shiver ran up his arm. Must be the wind, but he stared at where she touched him.

She yanked her hand away as if burned. She smelled of a confusing combination of shock and arousal.

Before either of them could make anything of a simple touch, he grabbed her by the gloved hand and pulled her into the forest. Deeper and deeper, to give them some distance from the others sensitive ears.

"That's far enough, Alistair. I want to be able to find them again."

He raised his eyebrows. "We just follow our scents back to them."

"Oh…" She shrugged. "Look, Pallas assigned me as team leader."

He shoved his cold hands into his pockets. "And?"

She sighed. "I know you mean well, but you're being selfish by ordering my team around."

"Your team is never going to survive without direction." He didn't understand why her words stung so much. For the first time, he was really trying to help others, for their sake and not his, yet she was upset. He rubbed the ache growing in his chest. "You might get hurt, Penny. I joined to protect you," he whispered.

Couldn't she grasp that?

Penny crossed her arms. "Ian made you volunteer. I'm not stupid."

"It's not like he twisted my arm. I mean, look at your team choices." He pointed back at the campsite. "Seriously? I haven't been here long, but from what I gather Pallas doesn't care if any of you die. Don't think I didn't notice that unmarked grave you visit on the edge of the property."

She gasped. Her eyes wide and brimming with tears. "Jake didn't die in training. It was from a house fire the

Penny of the Paranormal

humans had set. Not anything Pallas did."

"That doesn't excuse him almost drowning both Clare and Darrell or any of the other close calls others had suffered. You can still die out here."

"I'll have you know I picked the perfect team. Parker can build, Vicki can cook, Bobby Jo was studying to be an astronomer, Amy is a nurse and Nick, well… Nick is a florist but he can shift the fastest."

Alistair gave her a slow and meaningful glare. "You picked them with all this in mind."

"No, of course not. I didn't know that the mission would be a death march into a winter wonderland, but I can work with who I picked. If I recall properly, I didn't pick you." She jabbed him in the chest with a tiny little finger. Very un-omega like. But was it? She was protecting her team. Wasn't that the scope of omegas? To care for the pack. "I need a team. That means working together. My question is what do *you* offer us besides your opinions?"

Annie Nicholas

Hurt flashed through him as if she slapped him with claws out. He leaned forward until they shared air. "I can hunt." He was filled with inner demons, none of which he would share with Penny. She didn't need to know what drove him to take care of her.

She visibly swallowed. "Well, then, that can be helpful too." She spun around and stomped back to the camp—in the right direction, at least.

He kept his distance, least she heard his chuckles. He wasn't laughing because he'd won the argument. On the contrary, he thought he had lost it. The little omega had taken back control of her team without shedding one drop of blood. That was why he was laughing. At himself, for thinking he could just take over.

When he arrived at the campsite, he stopped dead in his tracks. Well, he'd be a donkey's uncle. Parker had built a lean-to and lined the snowy ground with evergreens to help retain their warmth. He crouched, peeking inside.

Penny of the Paranormal

They were all piled together with no room for him.

Penny was in the center of everyone, her gaze steady on his as if daring him to squeeze inside.

He sighed and curled up on the edge. This would be the worst time of his life and the girl he'd made this sacrifice for hated him now.

CHAPTER FOUR

The scent of smoke clogged Penny's nose. She couldn't breathe. Heat scorched her skin as she crawled on hands and knees. The manor was on fire again. Something struck her hands and she stumbled. It was a body. Her heart leaped to her throat. The smoke cleared and Jake's dead eyes stared back at her.

Penny jerked awake, a scream on the edge of her lips. Every muscle in her body was stiff and it took two tries to crawl over the bodies of her teammates and out of the lean-to. She sucked in a big lung full of cold air as if she'd actually been suffocating.

She hadn't known Jake long, only a few days, before the fire had taken his young life. He'd been the only omega male she'd ever met. It had been nice to have someone who seemed to

Penny of the Paranormal

understand her. They'd buried him on the manor's grounds since his pack refused to claim his body. That was how much an omega's life was worth to most packs. If he'd been a hunter, she bet they would have sent a delegation.

The cold had worked its way deep into her bones while she had slept, even with the body heat of the others to keep her warm. Then again, it could have been the nightmare that chilled her. She rose to her feet and peered through the dim morning sunlight and spun a slow circle. Where was the sun rising? The overcast sky and the trees made it difficult to judge east. Damn it. She'd placed her hopes on this so they could at least hike in the right direction.

Alistair strode out of the woods. Shoulders rolling as he walked in the way predators of her race did. It shouldn't be legal to look that sexy after spending a night sleeping in the snow. The wind tussled his hair and he gave her a lazy smile. "East is that way." He pointed in the direction he'd come from.

Annie Nicholas

"I know." It was a lie but he was probably too far to smell it.

The others were starting to stir.

"Where were you?" she whispered as he brushed past.

"Checking the perimeter. Looking for tracks or scents of prey. Marking my territory." At the last comment, he winked.

Her bladder decided to pick that moment to remind her she had her own territory to mark. She squeezed her thighs together. He seemed so calm and relaxed in the wild. Not like when he'd been stuck healing in the manor. There he always seemed on edge and filled with anger. She envied his relaxed confidence in the face of possible travesty.

Hurrying into the bushes, she found a secluded spot to take care of business. Unlike Alistair, she didn't flourish in the wild. She loved the forest and had grown up following the hunts her father organized until their lands had been taken from her pack by the banks. Her wolf senses came to life out here, but

Penny of the Paranormal

sadness tugged at her soul at those fleeting memories of her childhood. The expanse of the trees made her feel small and she never knew exactly what she was supposed to be doing. Like the whole hunting thing was a mysterious secret that no one had explained.

Once done, she strolled around the camp to see if she saw anything track-like. Why? She wasn't sure. Alistair had done it and he made it sound like it was the right thing to do.

"Penny?" Vicki joined her. "What are you doing?"

"Checking the perimeter and looking for prey." Glancing past Vicki, she spotted Alistair in the trees. His shoulders shook in silent laughter. Penny rolled her eyes at herself. What was she doing pretending to be a hunter? If a squirrel jumped out, she would probably scream from surprise.

"That's a good idea. I'm so starved I'd eat whatever you caught raw." Vicki clutched her stomach.

Penny's was filled with terrible pangs as well.

Alistair stopped mid-step, all signs of his amusement gone. "With your permission, Penny, I'll hunt while you and the others travel toward Mount Killmore."

"How will you find us?" Or was he using hunting as an excuse to escape the mission? He could always claim he wasn't able to find them and return to the manor. She couldn't blame him as she tried to stop her teeth from clacking together. But if he did leave them, he'd lose his bet with Pallas and lose a year of his life to working at the boot camp.

Alistair tapped his nose. "I'll track your scent and I don't plan on ranging too far." He pulled his sweater over his head.

Vicki's eyes went wide and Penny fought the urge to tell her to shut them. Nudity wasn't an issue for shifters, but Alistair had the best chest. All hard planes and masculine hair. A perfect place for a woman to rest her head. Before now she'd been the only one to see him without clothes and Penny didn't want to share this part of Alistair with anyone.

With a fingertip, Penny encouraged Vicki to close her mouth.

Alistair packaged his clothes into a neat bundle onto Vicki's arms. "Can you carry this for me?"

"S-sure." Vicki clutched his clothes as if it were a prize.

A nauseous, unexplainable feeling punched Penny in the gut. Her wolf rose, which was startling. Unlike others, her animal instincts flared when someone was in need, not for fighting or dominance. But she really wanted to slap that silly grin off Vicki's face.

Hurt, she turned her back on them and strode to the shelter, but Alistair blocked her escape route. He lowered his lips to hers.

She went still. Shocked at the gesture. He held her gaze and she was transfixed, helpless to react. Angling his head, he pressed his mouth against hers. She was surprised how soft his lips were. He was a hard man who filled the area around him with dominance. His kiss should have been demanding, but it wasn't. He plucked at her mouth with tiny, sexy smacking sounds until she leaned into him and stood on her tiptoes. His tongue brushed over her closed lips and a delicious rumble filled his chest.

She made him do that.

"Take care of them," he whispered against her mouth. Then Alistair shifted to beast form, his body covered in golden fur. Werewolves could walk on their hind legs, but hunting was easier on four. He paced around the camp then hurried by, pressing his huge body against her legs in farewell.

Vicki sighed, still clutching his clothes. "That was so romantic."

Heat blistered Penny's cheeks. "Come on. Let's gather the others." She stormed back to the campsite where the team milled around the lean-to trying to stay warm. "While Alistair hunts, we'll hike until we reach the mountain. Gather any wood you can carry as we trek so we can make a fire tonight." The snow would get worst as they climbed to

Penny of the Paranormal

higher ground and she imagined kindling would get scarce.

The journey was more pleasant in the daylight, if not as cold. At least they could see better. It should make hunting easier for Alistair.

A lump formed in her throat as she recalled what they'd done. He hadn't just kissed her. He had claimed her in front of Vicki, who most likely had told everyone else on her team by now. Where had that come from? She'd assumed Ian had forced Alistair to join her team by using the incentive of winning Pallas's car. What if that had been all a pretense?

Such a simple thing, a kiss. Yet it had changed something in her. It made her want. That was a dangerous urge. Civilizations had fallen because of want. Now she desired more than she'd allowed herself to in years because life without love wasn't a real life after all.

What was she thinking? He'd done it as a tactic for power. If he could blind her with lust, then he could take over her team easily. Or that was what he probably thought. She wouldn't let him.

To distract her mind from thoughts of *what if*, she listened to her team discuss the wood craft Pallas had taught them, such as looking for moss on the tree trunks to confirm north, and as the sun rose higher behind the clouds, she kept their direction on track. Their steps grew harder as the land inclined. Obviously, they had reached the mountain's base. If it was the right mountain was still to be determined.

The overcast sky had darkened and the wind's bite more sharp. She sniffed, rubbing her numb nose. Her jacket kept her somewhat warm as long as she kept moving, but not eating for days left her legs trembling with each step.

She wasn't the only one with symptoms of flagging strength.

Nick collapsed against a tree trunk, resting his head, eyes close. "Is bark edible?"

"If you were a deer," responded Bobby Jo.

Penny of the Paranormal

"We'll rest here for a few minutes." Their breaks were becoming more frequent and longer. Their only hope was Alistair.

Vicki still clutched his clothes. "Maybe we should try hunting?" They hadn't seen Alistair since early that morning.

"You're welcome to try." Everything she knew about hunting was theoretical. They had grocery stores. Why would she kill something wild and free? She didn't have that urge as a shifter. Not that she wouldn't pounce on Thumper or Bambi right now. She just didn't have any practical experience to lead a hunt.

"Or we could tough it out and keep marching forward to our goal." She pointed up the mountain.

"I vote for food." Nick raised his hand.

"Food," repeated Parker.

So they were a democracy now. What did the history teachers say? They were three meals away from anarchy. She didn't have the strength to fight them and needed them to continue working as a team. Hunger did terrible things to people and worse things to shifters.

"We hunt for an hour and meet back here. Travel in pairs," she ordered.

The others stripped and changed to their beast form. She gathered their clothes, including Alistair's, and set them on a large fallen log cleared of snow. "One hour," she repeated.

They took off before she finished speaking. Penny would guard their belongings and act as the messenger between hunters. She'd done this job before in her old pack.

She strolled around the area, looking, you know, for a McDonald's sign flashing in the distance.

Her mouth watered. That thought hadn't helped. The last time she'd eaten fast food was the town's fall festival. She and Blain had stuffed themselves silly on corn dogs, popcorn, and deep fried Oreos. Oh, god, those were the days. She'd thought the boot camp had been brutal *then*.

Stepping over snow covered branches, she spotted an irregularity in the ground ahead. She paused, taking in her surroundings. The quiet was so deep it was almost suffocating. Scents of evergreen, dirt and fox swept past in the wind. She crept forward, suddenly nervous to be alone.

Weren't horror movies based on idiots like her?

Heart pounding, she kept forcing one leg in front of the other, faster and faster as recognition registered.

A trail in the deep snow.

She knelt next to it and studied the paw prints. Too big for a real wolf, so it had to be another team from the boot camp. She traced the outline. The print was so big it matched her hand's size. Only one shifter's wolf was that big.

Ian... The alpha team had all shifted to travel. That was a good idea, which was why Ian made such a great leader and she didn't, but her team *could* follow this trail to find their way.

Pallas only said to return with the flag. It wasn't a race of who got there first but who *could* get there.

Annie Nicholas

Something wet and heavy landed on her eyelashes. She blinked her vision clear. Snow. She held out her palms, watching the flakes melt. So pretty. It was falling heavier and heavier.

She glanced at the trail. Oh shit, the snow would cover it soon. She jumped to her feet and ran to where she'd left the team's clothes, all the while calling out their names.

She stood by the fallen log, her breath fogging the air as she tried to catch her breath. No one called back. A howl would do. They were probably too far to hear her. She wished Pallas had let them keep their cellphones. What had her father done when hunting? She'd always been too busy picking flowers and feeding birds—to his horror—to pay attention.

The wind blew through the branches, howling with the sudden gust.

Howling…

She'd always been good singing with the pack on full moon nights. Come to think of it, her new pack hadn't spent a single night serenading the moon.

Maybe it was more of a pack custom than a species one.

It had been a long time since she'd howled in her human form though. She couldn't shift since it would be too difficult to explain the trail and snow fall. Throwing back her head, she started low and slow, letting the sound build up in her lungs before calling out to her teammates.

Snow was starting to fall in heavy flakes. Alistair paused to watch a few flat past his muzzle. So pretty. He flexed his claws, digging them into the frozen ground.

The game in the area was slim pickings. He could only guess that the prey smelled a pack of werewolves traveling through their forest and had either run or hidden. He'd only caught two rabbits but they were still fat from summer grazing. It wouldn't leave them full but it might prevent Parker from gnawing off Vicki's leg.

A familiar sound filtered through the bare branches. The howl was distant and female. Not a sound of distress but a call to gather. He tilted his head, ears forward. That wasn't Julia's howl. He knew hers from pack events back home. He couldn't imagine Clare's voice being so lyrical.

Penny?

His heart skipped a beat. Why was she calling for the others? They were supposed to stick together. Why had they abandoned her? He grabbed the rabbits in his mouth and followed the distant sound. It was faint. They had covered more ground than he would have guessed. Maybe it wasn't Penny howling and he was running in the wrong direction. He paused every few minutes to search the ground for her scent.

On the third try, he finally caught her smell on a bush she must have brushed against.

CHAPTER FIVE

By the time Penny's team responded to her call, the snow was falling so thickly she had to shield her eyes to see their approach. She explained the trail that she wanted to follow before it was covered by snow.

She ordered them to stay in wolf form. Her team could move easier in this deep groundcover on their wide paws. Not to mention shifting took a lot of energy, something everyone was short on, but she stayed in human form to make communication easier.

The trail had a thin layer of snow on it but they could still follow the other team toward their goal—the flag on top of Mount Killmore.

Marching as a group, they climbed the steep slope. Each time Penny faltered, one of her teammates was at her side to steady her steps. She would move faster and be warmer if she shifted, but who would carry their gear? And secretly, she feared in wolf form she would revert to her omega role. It was more difficult to ignore instinct in her beast form.

Every few minutes, she paused to visually search the woods for Alistair's golden wolf. No such luck. He had promised to stay close but hadn't responded to her call. Was he lost or hurt?

The fourth time she stopped, Nick bumped her side to continue moving. His fur was matted with chunks of icy snow. Penny touched her hair and felt the ice forming on her braid. They couldn't continue in this blizzard or they'd freeze to death.

"We have to find shelter from the snow and wind," she shouted over the storm. Her teeth chattered, making her hard to understand.

In wolf form, Parker couldn't build them another lean-to. Not that such a shelter would work in this fierce

Penny of the Paranormal

weather. The wind was so sharp it cut through her layers of clothing right down to her bones.

The falling snow made visibility suck. The trail they were following zigzagged across the mountainside instead of going straight up the side, but she watched as Clare's team's tracks disappeared under the heavy snowfall. She hoped the others in the pack were safe, because they sure weren't.

"Okay," she called out. "Gather close, I don't want to lose anyone. We're changing direction and going straight up." It wasn't like Ian and Clare to take the easy route, so what had made them travel alongside the mountain?

The going was tough. Penny's legs trembled from the effort of climbing in the deep snow. Her team plowed ahead, clearing a path. Nausea rolled in her gut. Alistair was out in this weather all by himself. What if he froze? She couldn't bear the thought and focused on saving those around her.

Alistair had joined this mission to protect her and she had abandoned him.

Ahead, Amy came to a halt. Tail wagging, she turned around and barked.

Penny peered through the snowflakes lining her eyelashes. What was Amy excited about? A few more steps closer and she finally saw the cliff face had a nice overhang. Under it, the ground was covered in only a thin layer of snow.

"Thank God." She wearily made her way under and fell to her knees. Wrapped in her teams' clothing was the wood they had collected to make a fire. For once, she had made a good call. The kindling scattered across the frozen ground as she dumped her arm load.

With frozen fingers, she gathered what she needed to start a fire. She'd been making them since her arrival to boot camp but her hands were so numb that every time she tried to roll the stick between her palms to create friction, it tumbled free.

"Fuck." She picked up the stick for the third time. Shivers traveled through her whole body now.

"Here." Vicki stretched out her hand to take over.

Penny of the Paranormal

Penny had been so focused on starting a fire she hadn't noticed her team had all shifted and dressed.

Vicki made quick work of rolling the stick in her hand until a spark developed in the frozen wood. They work together to get the fire going, then huddled over the warm. Hands held out over the flame, Penny closed her eyes for just a second and listened to the pop and crackle of the burning wood. They might actually survive the night.

Bobby Jo put his arm around her shoulders. "Nice job. I was getting scared we would turn into wolf-sicles."

"Me too," chimed in Parker.

Penny shrugged out of Bobby Jo's hold and stared out into the storm. "Alistair is still out there alone."

Nick snorted. "He's probably safe in the manor by now."

"Why would you say that?" Though she had shared those same thoughts earlier. Something in her gut believed in Alistair.

"Because he's a self-serving asshole," was Nick's response.

A wolf was influenced by his or her pack. Only when separated could they truly expand their wings and find their true selves. The boot camp had proven this time and again. They had been training for weeks to find their true natures, though most of her pack mates didn't recognize what Pallas was truly doing. Alistair hadn't had the same amount of time, but every day she saw a spark inside of him grow stronger.

Kinder.

At least toward her. It was a start. She continued to gaze out through the storm, looking for a spark of gold.

Amy went out to gather more wood hidden under the snow. Their little overhang against the cliff kept in the heat and protected them against the wind and snow.

Guilt ate at Penny's soul. She rose to her feet. "I'm going to take a quick look around for Alistair." What if he was lying just outside their vision?

"Penny." Vicki grabbed her wrist. "Don't."

Penny of the Paranormal

"I won't go far. I promise." She pointed to the reflective cliff side. "Look, the firelight is like a beacon."

Reluctantly, Vicki released her hold. "Don't be long. We can't afford to be sending out rescue party after rescue party until we're all lost."

Penny smiled, doing her best to make it reassuring. "Don't worry."

Alistair started his journey enamored by snowflake. Now, he fucking hated every little unique flake. How did the snow accumulate so high when the particles were so fucking tiny? He was from Texas. The occasional light dusting was the most he had seen. He'd been hunting in Colorado in the past with his father, but the Lodge had never been too far away.

He *could* abandon his team and turn tail to find the manor. What could the vampire do to him for coming back for shelter, fail him?

No, no. Penny was out in this terrible blizzard. He couldn't leave the little wolf to freeze. First, he'd find her, then he'd drag her ass back to the manor by the scruff if he had to. The others could follow or not. This exercise was ridiculous. No matter what the vampire thought, shifters really could freeze to death. They weren't as resilient as Pallas wanted to believe.

The snow made tracking scents difficult, if not impossible. Luckily, his team left tracks wide enough that the most inexperienced hunter could follow. But if he didn't find them soon, the snow would bury their paw prints.

He paused, set the rabbits down, and howled. The dense snowfall muffled his call. He spun around. His own trail was fading. He shook his head clear of snowflakes. Which way was the manor?

Fuckity, fuck, fuck.

Lost, that was all he needed. First, he'd been shot by his ex-fiancée, now was lost in a snowstorm. He shook again to clear the cold snow from his body, but it stayed frozen to his fur. A wet hide meant less insulation from the weather. Frozen fur meant death. He needed shelter.

Penny of the Paranormal

Penny was experiencing the same weather. Had she even thought to shift to wolf form? As a human, he wouldn't have made it this far. He couldn't give up on her. It wasn't in his nature. She'd spent days caring for him even when they both knew he was healed and just needing some time to come to terms with his loss. She'd still checked on him, gave him food, hell, she'd given him *her* food when the vampire was starving the pack.

There was no way he was going to find shelter without making sure she was safe first.

He stumbled against a buried dead log. Maybe he should eat the rabbits. It was getting difficult to travel and carrying them didn't make it easier, especially with the snow covering all sorts of death traps like this log.

A faint scent was mixed with the deadwood. Parker, Vicki, Nick, Amy, and Bobby Jo. Penny too. *They been here!* He was on the right track. He would keep the rabbits then. It wasn't much but they would need the food to fuel their bodies.

Pushing forward, Alistair plowed through the snow. The land grew steeper and steeper. His heart raced. Maybe their bodies were covered in snow? The thought put more speed in his steps and he paused to dig when he spotted a wolf shaped snow pile.

There was nothing. He'd been mistaken and he paused to catch his breath. He was going to die on this godforsaken mountain. No one would ever find his body and his family would just assume he'd run away in shame since he'd lost Julia to a penniless wolf.

They'd never know that he hadn't cared for her. That he had hunted her down to the boot camp because they had pushed him. If he had really wanted Julia as a mate, he would have won the challenge against Darrell. His heart hadn't been in the fight.

Penny's scent filled his nose. It blew on the wind howling past his face. She was close. Ignited by the smell, he started his frozen march again. Between the trees of the steep mountain side, a flicker of light caught his attention. A flashlight? He kept climbing, unable to move any faster on frozen paws. There it was again. Brighter, more orange than artificial light.

A fire!

It must be Penny and her team. His heart soared and he climbed with his muzzle still full of dead rabbit.

Firelight coated the cliff face with an overhang protecting the team from the blizzard.

Parker and Nick rose to their feet as he approached. "Is Penny with you?"

CHAPTER SIX

Alistair dropped the rabbits at Vicki's feet and scanned the weary team's faces. Penny wasn't among them?

Ears back, he paced around the fire, a low growl rumbling in his chest. They had lost Penny? He faced the thick snowfall outside the protection of the overhang. The sun had set and it was dark. It would only get colder. He shifted and dressed, jerking on his clothes in sharp fast moves. "Why isn't Penny here with you, safe by the fucking fire?"

Vicki knelt next to him. "She went out to look for you. We try to stop her but she insisted she wouldn't go far. That was two hours ago."

"We've been going out in pairs to look for her. Me and Nick just returned." Parker's blue lips flattened in distress. "I'm really worried she's lost."

Penny of the Paranormal

Alistair bared his teeth. He wanted to bite him. All of them. How could they let her leave the safety of the team for someone like him?

They both shrank back to the other side of the fire with the rest of their teammates.

The ache in his chest was unbearable. He had thought he had found her. "It's not your fault. It's mine. Stay by the fire in case she finds her way back. We can't afford to lose anyone else in this storm. I'll find her." She was lost in the blizzard because of him. He told her he would track them after his hunt.

How could he blame her for not believing in him? He had had his own doubts when looking for her.

He pushed the rabbits toward the hungry shifters. "You need to eat to stay warm." And he raced out back into the storm.

They had tried to find her, he reminded himself, but they failed. He wouldn't.

Ian had asked him to watch over Penny. The alpha must have suspected the vampire was planning something dangerous. If he had known the weather would turn, Alistair would have dragged her back to the manor no matter the consequences to her training or his bet with Pallas.

A year of work was nothing to pay in comparison to saving her life.

The wind sliced through Alistair's jacket sending shivers through his body. Wolf form would be warmer and he could travel faster but he didn't need speed. He needed to be able to call out for Penny since visibility was nil. He hoped she had shifted before searching for him. Their fur was more resilient than clothes.

He followed the vanishing trail Penny and the others had made until it split off in different directions. Snow washed out their smells. He could discern Parker and Nick but not Penny. Snarling in frustration, Alistair scanned the terrain.

If he were Penny, looking for him, what direction would he go?

Not up the mountain—he'd been behind them, on lower ground. He

Penny of the Paranormal

twisted around and couldn't see the firelight from the team's sheltered spot through the snowfall and the scent of smoke had faded. He hadn't gone that far. Shit, she could be a few feet from him and he wouldn't see her. No wonder she'd gotten lost. He thought he was too.

He threw back his head and shouted her name. He may not be able to see her but maybe *she* could hear him. If she would only call back.

Nothing.

He ran farther down the mountainside, leaping over fallen trees and ducking low branches. Pausing again, he caught his breath before letting out another call.

Come on, come on.

Now, he was running and calling her name. Make enough noise to scare all the game in a ten-mile radius away. His breath no longer steamed from his mouth—body temperature must be dropping—legs wobbling…

Maybe he should just lay down here for a minute and catch his breath. He plopped against a snowbank and closed his eyes. So tired…

Something brushed his hand. It felt nice, like little fingers. Little ice cold fingers.

A jolt ran through his limbs as he rolled to his feet, heart pounding in his ears.

Penny lay buried in the snow. She reached out to him in zombie style. Of all things, she was still in her human form. He wanted to shout and yell at her. He wanted to kiss and hold her tight. He wanted to rage at the world.

Instead, he grabbed her by the scruff of her jacket and pulled her into his arms, squeezing her tight. "You're safe now."

She was alive.

He carried her as he climbed back up the mountain even though every muscle in his body seemed frozen solid.

She was alive.

That was all that mattered. Penny had spent days saving him from depression that had threatened to engulf him whole. He'd gone from alpha heir apparent to rejected mate. His pack would never accept him back after such a defeat. Shot in the leg by his own promised female, he would be lucky if they didn't tear him apart. Whenever the darkness seemed the worst, like the sun would never rise again, Penny appeared to bring light back into his life. A moment of silver lining in an otherwise cloudy world.

Failure wasn't an option. She would survive because a world without Penny in it was too dark for Alistair to live in.

"You came for me," she whispered by his ear, burying her face against his neck. "I can't believe you came for me." He felt her sob and his heart broke.

Of course he'd found her. Why would she doubt him?

He paused, searching the falling curtain of snow for firelight or the scent of smoke, but found nothing. "Shit." Maybe he'd spoken too soon when he'd declared her safe because he was good and lost. He'd been following his own footsteps but the snow was coming down so hard his trail had vanished further up the mountain. He had nothing to guide him except to continue forward.

Penny had gone limp in his arms. Her body no longer shivered as if it had given up on trying to stay warm. No food for days, she just didn't have the reserve to combat the cold.

She was the only person he'd met that never asked anything of him and she was the only person he would do anything for.

"Stay with me, beautiful. I'll find us some shelter. Just hang on." Step after agonizing step, he lost track of time. His windblown face was numb. He could no longer feel his toes or fingers. The only thing that kept him going was the woman in his arms.

"Pallas." She stirred and lifted her nose to the air.

Alistair stumbled to a stop. "Where?" He searched the dark. The vampire would be a welcome sight for once.

"Smell." She pointed toward a thick copse of trees.

He inhaled deeply a few times, mouth open to increase the absorption of the

Penny of the Paranormal

surrounding scents. She was right. He could smell the vampire, if faintly. Following the smell, Alistair carried Penny into the denser area of trees and came to a sudden halt.

"You must have a guardian angel." Alistair stared at a small cabin. No lights were on or smoke from the chimney.

"Jake," she whispered.

Alistair frowned at the unfamiliar name, citing a surge of possessiveness. A boyfriend, possibly?

There was no answer when he knocked and the door was locked. With one swift kick, he broke the lock. Breaking and entering was not the worst offense he'd ever committed. Considering the situation, the police might be lenient.

He shoved the door closed with his shoulder and set Penny on a chair. "I'll get a fire started."

Most hunters kept their cabins stocked with the basics. Never knew when an emergency would strike, especially in unpredictable mountain weather.

Firewood was stacked by the hearth and he fumbled in the dark along the mantel looking for a lighter. Instead, he found a box of matches.

Pallas's scent was everywhere, faded with time. The vampire had used this cabin in the last week. Probably when he set the flags on top of the peak.

It took Alistair a few tries with his trembling hands but he finally started the fire.

Penny shuffled over, falling against his lap as she hurried toward the heat. Her teeth chattered, lips were blue and her eyelashes were iced over. She looks like an ice fairy, so beautiful and fierce. "Where is our team?"

"I left them at the cliff face with a couple of fat rabbits." His stomach rumbled at the memory and Penny's answered in kind. He twisted around, inspecting the cabin in the flickering fire light.

A bed with blankets, thick curtains over the windows to block the sunlight, table with chairs. Very basic hunter's cabin. Not really something he pictured

Penny of the Paranormal

the vampire owning. Alistair strode around the small space searching the cabinets.

"Bingo." He pulled out a couple of cans. "Beans."

Definitely not the vampire's cabin. He hadn't any need for food. Didn't mean he hadn't used the place to hide from the sun for a day.

Penny clapped her hands. "I can eat it, metal and all."

After a few agonizing minutes, Alistair found the can opener. "No need to add tin to our diet." He set the open cans in the coals burning in the fireplace to warm the frozen contents.

Penny dipped her fingers inside the closest one. "I can eat mine cold. I don't mind."

"Careful, don't cut yourself on the sharp edge." Alistair gently pulled her arm away. "Leave them in the heat. You'll get warm faster if your stomach is filled with hot food."

She moaned and leaned against his chest. "I have never been this hungry before."

His inner hunter rose and he regretted leaving the rabbits with the team. Meat would satisfy her wolf better than beans. A soft frustrated rumble emanated from his chest. Penny shouldn't suffer. Gentle wolves like her were meant to be cared for by the pack.

The feel of her in his arms soothed his raging wolf. Most packs didn't agree with his beliefs though. Many mistreated their omegas, including his own pack. No matter what the others said, his motivation for wanting to become alpha was to change his pack's attitude. That possibility was gone now.

The beans bubbled in the cans and he pulled them free of the coals.

Using her gloves, Penny held her hot tin to her mouth and drank down the warm meal.

He offered her his can.

She gave him a slow blink. "I'm full." Then a shy smile bloomed on her sweet lips. "You must be starved after running all over the mountain."

Penny of the Paranormal

He was, but he could endure the hunger a little longer. It would actually make him a better hunter. "I'm good."

She pushed his full can away. "I need you to stay strong and not go feral on me." Sighing, her shoulders slumped. "We would have been dead without you."

"No, you would have found a way. You're very resourceful." He ate his meal almost as quickly as Penny. The cold had taken a toll on his strength and the food was welcomed. "You should have stayed with the others. You could have died out there."

"You could have died too." She sniffed. "I couldn't just abandon you. I thought you were lost."

He gathered her hands in his. It grew harder to breathe as their gazes locked. "I never realized how lost I was until now."

Chapter Seven

Alistair's icy hands warmed Penny's heart. He'd almost frozen to death trying to find her. His words though set her on fire.

"You're no longer lost, I found you," she whispered.

"You rescued me. Everyone else wrote me off—they think I'm useless. Thank you for not assuming that."

She recalled how hurt he'd looked last night in the woods when she called him selfish and shame burned her cheeks. "I'm sorry about what I said to you last night."

"You don't have to apologize." His attention dipped to the fire and he seemed unable to meet her gaze again. "Everyone thinks that. I'm used to it."

She brushed her fingertips over his flushed cheeks, stubble scratched her cold skin. She knew how it felt to be

Penny of the Paranormal

misjudged by others. To be different. "You're a good wolf, Alistair." His hair was a mess from the wind and she ran her fingers through the silken strands until they were smooth.

As she pulled away, he grabbed her wrist so fast she jumped. He pressed her hand to his left cheek. "I like it when you touch me."

"I like touching you." More than she thought possible. She'd never sought out a mate, always guarded her heart because most wolves thought of omegas as disposable. Alistair's reaction to her was empowering. He made her feel wanted and in control.

"I'm sorry I ridiculed your team choices." He leaned into her touch. "You have a unique way of seeing the best in people. I only seem to see the worst." He shrugged. "They took turns looking for you in the storm."

She gasped. "I hope they're still not trying." She couldn't bear losing another friend.

"No, I ordered them to stay put by the fire. It's too easy to get lost in the storm and I can't spend the whole night looking for everyone." He chuckled but it lacked mirth. "They're good team members. I think a group of more dominant hunters wouldn't have worked so well together."

His compliment meant a lot. He wasn't the type to give them unless he truly believed a person deserved it. She knew Alistair's story. Rich, powerful pack, and he was their heir but something didn't make sense. "Why did you make that wager with Pallas?"

He could lose a whole year of his life to her taskmaster and she was sure Pallas wouldn't make it an easy time. Alistair didn't need a car. He had a Porsche parked in front of the manor. None of it made sense. Even if Ian had asked him to join for her sake, Alistair didn't owe him anything.

He just gazed at her as if waiting.

"What?" She tilted her head and crept a little closer. "You can tell me. I'm good at keeping secrets."

He shook his head in disbelief. "You really have no clue." He cupped her chin

Penny of the Paranormal

in the palm of his hand and ran his thumb over her bottom lip.

Her heartbeat pounded painfully in her chest. "Me?" That was the most difficult question she'd ever asked. She'd admired him from afar, never even daydreaming he might return her interest.

What if she was wrong? The embarrassment alone at his rejection had the potential to shred her. She bowed her head, unable to meet his stare. Her eyes burned. How horrifying. She'd fallen for Alistair Montgomery Carrington the Third and just admitted it to his face.

"What sort of wolf would I be to let the woman I care for out into the wilderness without me?"

With a shaky hand, she pressed her fingertips to his lips to silence him, unable to hear anymore. This strong hunter wanted her. He smelled of snow, smoke, and pine mixed to make a heady, sexy scent. It was earthy and masculine, just like Alistair. She wanted to open a window to relieve the pressure in her lungs. Her wolf wanted to roll in his musk. Bite him. Claim him. Take him.

"What are you thinking?" His eyes look sad and tired, like all the life was draining from him.

"That you're crazy to care for someone like me." What could he possibly see in her? Meek, soft, emotional mess. These weren't mate qualities for such a strong shifter. He deserved a confident female at his side. "I'm just an omega."

He pulled her fingers from his mouth. "You bring out the best in me, Penny. You make me want to surpass everyone's expectations of me. I've never met anyone like you." He pressed his lips over hers in a chaste kiss then let her go. "I just needed you to know that. I don't care about the car or winning." He laughed. "I don't even care about working for Pallas. You say the word and we'll gather the others and march back to the manor first thing in the morning."

"No." She wasn't sure what she was denying. Quitting, failing boot camp, or

Alistair losing a year? All of it, probably. One thing was for sure, she didn't like him pulling away from their kiss.

The walls around her heart were strong and thick, but that single tender kiss had shattered them. She'd never dared dream of falling in love. Not even when she cared for him while he was injured.

"Oh no, you don't." She crawled onto his lap. "You don't say things like that and then get to pull away." Her heart beat against her chest as his eyes dipped to her lips. Her breath froze as he leaned closer.

"You want me to kiss you again, don't you?" His voice was impossibly low and sexy. Fire light and shadow highlighted his gorgeous cheekbones and amber eyes.

Her lips throbbed with wanting and her heart stirred as if waking from a long slumber. Everything would be different. She wanted that.

Searching his eyes, she nodded. The heat in her cheeks flamed harder.

Adoration pooled in his eyes. Nothing possessive or dominating like the other males in her old pack.

Alistair leaned his forehead against Penny's and closed his eyes. His breathing was ragged. He pressed his lips to hers, once, twice. Two little kisses that felt like he was trying to talk himself out of going deeper with her.

He was scared. The realization rocked her. He was just as scared of what was growing between them as she was.

This was huge. Earth shattering.

Angling her chin, she returned his kisses just as gently. Lips moving slowly against his, she wrapped her legs around his hips.

A rumble rolled in his chest. Throaty, content and practically purring in pleasure. The noise grew louder as he gripped her ass and rocked his erection against her. He opened her mouth and brushed his tongue against hers. His hand twisted in her hair while the other ran down along her back to the base of her spine. He pulled her closer and thrust his tongue deeper in her mouth.

Penny of the Paranormal

Holy moly, Alistair was sexy, but this was more than she hoped for. He adjusted her hips and hit right where her sensitive clit was pressed against his groin.

Alistair trailed kisses from her mouth, along her jaw, and down her neck.

The heat from the fire had warmed the small cabin though it didn't compare to what Alistair did to her.

His fingers trailed under the hem of her sweater, setting wing to the butterflies in her stomach. He continued along her rib cage and back down again as shivers of pleasure coursed through her body.

Despite the raging storm outside, she was growing hot. She took off her jacket and eagerly pressed her hands to his sculpted chest. Together they were creating their own inferno.

Braver than she'd ever felt, she pulled off her sweater and undid her bra. Alistair made her feel safe. She'd never met a dominant hunter who didn't frighten her on some level. Deep down inside, she knew he would never do anything to hurt her.

She wanted nothing more than to rub their bare flesh together, to share their burning warmth, and burrow against him until they were one.

Alistair's lips parted as she shrugged out of her bra. Then he reverently cupped her breasts. She closed her eyes and released the breath she'd been holding. Her exhale turned into a moan as he rolled her erect nipples with his thumbs.

His hands were rough and he contrasted to her smooth skin. Alistair eased her back onto the pile of their sweaters and coats, cupping the back of her head as she arched against him. He dipped his mouth, captured the tip of her breast and pulled on her sensitive nipple.

Penny was wet by the time he moved to her other breast. She rolled her hips in rhythm to his sucking and bowed against him. She was so close to coming and they still hadn't taken off their jeans.

Penny of the Paranormal

"Oh," she whispered as he nipped her breast. Her breath was ragged as pressure built between her thighs.

Alistair yanked on the button of her jeans. The zipper fought him for a second before coming undone. His hand was warm as he slid it under her panties and cupped her sex. "You're so soft," his voice was rough with emotion.

She pulled his face toward hers, kissing him with desperate hunger. She'd thought she'd been starved for food earlier but it didn't compare to how she craved his touch. Each time she moved her hips, he slid his finger deeper inside of her. Whimpering noises were wrenched from her throat.

He pressed her to the floor with the weight of his huge, muscular body, deepening their kiss as she bucked against his hand.

Helpless noises rolled between their lips. All worries melted from her thoughts. Only this moment between her and Alistair existed. She'd never surrendered herself so completely to a lover. She'd lay back and let them have her, but Alistair didn't take anything from her.

He only gave.

"Alistair," she moaned, breaking from the kiss and gripping his biceps, suddenly unsure how to ride the wave of ecstasy surging over her.

He pressed harder onto her clit and set her off.

The orgasm stole her breath away. Every muscle in her body clenched. Her hands on his arm, nails biting into his hard muscles. Her legs around his hips. Her insides around his fingers.

He kissed her, long languid kisses, as if savoring her lips as the aftershocks subsided. He kissed her until her body wanted more of him.

All these years, she'd never really known what she'd been missing. Now, she knew what it was to be with someone who cared about her. How could she ever go back to her old pack and just be something that was used?

He'd wrecked her. He'd released her. He'd awakened her. He made her want more from her life.

Penny of the Paranormal

"Penny," he whispered against her lips. He sounded devastated. "It's not a good idea for us to bond. You deserve better."

"I have no regrets." She combed her fingers through his thick hair. "And you're better than you think." She shimmied out of her jeans and panties.

His gaze raked over her naked form. "You don't play fair." He met her gaze. His eyes were serious and hard. "You sure you want this? I'm a hot mess and I don't play well with others."

Her stomach churned with a surge of possibilities. What was happening between them felt right. She must have sensed that since they met. No matter what happened from now on, she knew she could count on Alistair. He'd always have her back. She wasn't some one night stand to him.

She ducked her chin. "I want you." Scrunching her nose, she couldn't ignore the flame of embarrassment covering her cheeks. "I've never allowed myself to want anyone before." She hated being so exposed to another person but she needed him to understand that this meant something to her as well.

When she finally raised her chin to meet his stare, his eyes were wide with wonder.

He shucked off his pants. "Come here."

She couldn't move. The man was a demigod in the flesh. Strong, sculpted muscles lined his limbs, shaft long and thick, and an alluring dusting of hair on his chest. Her wolf growled in approval. Penny ran her finger along the silken skin of his erection. He was all man and predator rolled into one scrumptious shifter.

A ravenous noise came from him as she grabbed him by the base and stroked upward. He was so strong and confident yet with her so gentle and loving. He listened when she spoke and saw her. Really, really saw her as a woman and not a weak link in the pack.

He crawled on top of her, stroking a hand from her collarbone, between the valley of her breasts, to her navel. "You smell good. The scent of your arousal is

Penny of the Paranormal

driving me mad. I love that I do that to you." He nipped her ear lobe then ducked to graze his teeth over her neck.

She wrapped him in her limbs, knees around his ribs, arms circling his neck. "Take me." She was ready to be filled

His breathing grew erratic as he teased her opening with his tip. "I want you so bad." The growling in his throat started again. Such a sexy, dangerous noise. He kissed her long and deep, rocking his hips to slide his tip inside of her.

In and out, he moved as if she would break.

Desperate, she clawed his back. "More, please more." She didn't need a gentle lover. She wanted him wild and out of control.

As if his reserve was dissolving with her plea, he bucked into her, filling her completely.

"Harder," she cried and bit his shoulder.

A feral cry tore from his throat as he threw back his head, eyes hooded with dark desire. "Do that again."

She grinned and released her bite only to repeat it on his chest.

"Yes," he groaned and grabbed her ass. Drawing out again, he thrust inside her, picking up his pace. His powerful hips pushed into her harder and faster. He was potent, his touch consumed her. She threw back her head and called out his name as another orgasm pounded through her.

Alistair grunted as his warmth splashed into her, his thrusts erratic as he came. He slowed and just held her, kissing the tip of her nose with his eyes closing.

Feelings she'd thought impossible sprang to life. Instincts bubbled to the surface. Things like *mine, mine, mine* chanted in her head.

He pulled out of her and rolled off, only to return with a damp wash cloth from the tiny kitchen. He spread her legs.

"What are you doing?" She leaned up on her elbows.

"Taking care of you." He wiped along her sex and inner thighs. Once done, he

Penny of the Paranormal
pulled on her panties and jeans then helped with her bra. "I don't want you to get cold again." He dressed and pulled her into his arms by the fire and pressed kisses on her cheeks. Pulling her close to his chest, he stroked her mussed hair. She couldn't recall the last time she'd felt so safe and warm.

CHAPTER EIGHT

The snowfall was glorious. The way to transform the world to black and white, no gray areas, just the occasional evergreen tree and the rare red berry to break the monotony.

Pallas geared down his sports car as he took the sharp curve in the empty road. Driving this late at night was pure pleasure. Nobody to slow him down, the powerful purr of his baby pulling him along at speeds he had only imagined, and the crisp winter air blowing through his open windows. It was as close to flying as he'd ever get.

His wolves were probably not having near as much fun in the weather, being warm-blooded animals. Yet they were animals and they needed a little reminder of how powerful they were in times of need.

Penny of the Paranormal

He couldn't have planned this hiking trip any better if he had tried. Starved, cold, and stressed—the three catalysts every wolf feared. These modern day packs were soft. What had Ian called it? First world problems. That was all they were faced with until now. After this weekend such things would be insignificant.

Perspective. That was what he was teaching his wolves.

He grinned as the tires slid in the back and fish tailed around the next turn. Close one. He didn't want to scratch the paint job. He'd just gotten her back from the detailers.

A sparkle of color in his rearview mirror caught his attention.

Lights. Red and blue…

The siren's blare finally reached his ears.

He sighed. The local police.

Again.

He swore they parked in the woods along this road just to give him tickets. He thought he banked their payroll at this point. He took the next turn, driving on a dirt road leading to an easement on his land. His car could manage the terrain, but maybe not so fast. It was built for speed and not rough ground.

The police car followed, pulling close to his fender.

He'd have to speak with the sheriff about her staff harassing him. The wheel jerked in his hand as he hit an unseen bump covered in the snow. His car spun until he was face to face with his pursuer.

Their gazes locked.

Sheriff Lee.

Her eyebrows furrowed and her lips flattened. He could almost hear her steering wheel creak under her grip as she leaned forward.

He waved before the spin pulled him away and sent his car into a ditch.

Pallas blinked. Something sticky caked his eyelashes. Running his hands over his eyes, he tried to clear his vision. Red, white, and blue lights flashed against his shattered windshield. Was he having a weird patriotic dream? He didn't tend to dream of the night. Most of them took place in the daylight in the woods with his family.

The ringing in his ears wouldn't go away and was giving him the worst headache. Blood coated his hands. A snack? He sniffed and grimaced. Maybe not. This was his nasty blood. He was bleeding.

Fuck that ringing.

The driver side door of his car squealed open. How had he gotten into the passenger seat?

Wait a minute.

How had he gotten into his car?

"Pallas!" Sheriff Lee crawled into his car. Normally in his dreams her uniform was much tighter with the buttons of her shirt straining to pop.

He fingered the one between her breasts but it remained fastened.

She swatted his hand away. "What the fuck?" Then her eyes went wide. "Your jaw looks broken. Don't move. I'll call nine-one-one." She pulled out her cell phone.

He blinked again as his brain damage healed. His car… His baby… He yanked the phone from her hand and hung up. Moaning, he waved her out of the vehicle—his poor sweet little car— but there could be fuel leaking. He could fix his car, make her new. Sheriff Lee was much more vulnerable.

She slipped under his arm, supporting his weight, all the while muttering things under her breath like *stubborn*, *dumbass*, and *idiot*.

That last name stung. She had been the one chasing him, after all.

She set him on a snow bank next to her police car and went inside to turn off the siren. The ringing in his ears finally stopped. She returned, kneeling next to him.

"About time." He clutched his aching head, but his words came out muffled and the pain in his face grew sharper. He ran his fingertips over his disfigured jaw. Had to set it before the bones healed this way. With a jerk, he reset his mouth back in place.

Penny of the Paranormal

The sheriff gasped, a look of horror on her face. "You shouldn't do that."

He held up his hand and closed his eyes as the pain faded to a dull roar and his bones knitted back together.

Once again she had her phone in her hand. "Send an ambul—"

He pulled the phone from her ear. "I'm fine," he reported the operator. "She's just being dramatic." He ended the call and handed her back the cell phone. "Exactly what do you expect a doctor can do for me? Open a vein and let me feed?"

She tried to stand but slipped in the snow and ended up sitting face-to-face with him. "Your jaw is healed."

He pumped his arms and legs, checking for other injuries. All seemed intact. Good. Growing limbs took time.

Sheriff Lee looked pale.

Tilting his head, he met her wide-eyed stare. "You do realize I'm a real vampire? Not some bloke pretending to be one."

Her face morphed from shock to something akin to fury. She smacked him upside the head. "Of course."

"Ouch. I just smashed that against the windshield. Try to be a little gentler." He rubbed the spot where she had just assaulted him.

"That could have been avoided if you were following the speed limit." She gestured to his crashed car.

Now that his vision was clear, he could see the front end had accordioned against a tree. How was he going to keep his brother, Daedalus, from finding out? One more condescending conversation from him and Pallas would reconsider his decision to stay in this age of technology. He rested his arms on his knees. Cars were the main temptation to remain awake. Speed and oil and leather.

"You could have killed someone."

"How?" He tongued his teeth. They didn't feel aligned right.

She made a noise that sounded like multiple sentences starting at the same time.

Penny of the Paranormal

"Sheriff, I drive this late at night because no one is on the roads in the small town." The area was populated by farmers and he was a vampire. They didn't keep the same schedule. "What are you doing up so late? Shouldn't sheriffs have better work hours?"

She crossed her arms. "There were complaints of you speeding along here late at night." She grimaced. "The other officers didn't feel comfortable stopping you alone."

"Wise of them." He gave her a meaningful look and glanced at his wrecked vehicle. "How will my insurance company contact yours?"

"You can't believe this is my fault."

"Your sirens distracted my concentration. I've driven this road many times without a problem."

"It hasn't stormed this hard since you moved to the area." Her gaze returned to his jaw and she ran her hand along his chin. "Do you always heal this fast?"

"Faster if I'm well fed." Her touch stirred something dead inside of him. It burned.

She jerked her hand away and rose to her feet. "I'll call for a tow truck." From her pocket, she pulled out a pad of paper, tore a sheet loose and handed it over.

"What is this?" He read over it. "Speeding ticket?" When he looked up she was already in her vehicle backing away from his accident.

Well, fuck. Guesses wolves weren't the only ones hiking in the storm tonight.

CHAPTER NINE

The sunlight didn't break through the thick curtains but Alistair sensed the morning and groaned against awakening. Penny's warm form lay cuddled against his chest and he didn't want to venture out into the cold yet.

Their fire was only embers and they'd used the last of the firewood. Penny shouldn't roll out from under their blanket to an ice cold cabin, but what could he do? He eyed the sparse furniture. With his strength, he could snap those chairs into kindling.

Penny stretched beside him. "Good morning, lover."

The pet name warmed him like no fire could. He rolled, pulling her into a kiss. Her lips swollen and sweet from last night's lovemaking. Things were different with her. His past partners had always wanted something from him. It was how things worked in his pack. All Penny wanted was him. Selfish, stubborn, prideful him. He didn't want to be those things anymore though. He would strive to be the wolf she deserved.

She ran her fingers through his hair and melted into his arms. "Now that's how I want to wake up every morning." She pulled him in for a quick chaste kiss. "But we need to find the others and make sure they're okay."

He tilted his head. "And if they aren't?"

"We bring them back here, silly." Without hesitation, she rolled out from under the warm covers and dressed. "We could break the chairs for wood if we have to."

He grinned as her words echoed his earlier thoughts, but his concern was for her and hers was for everyone else. A true omega. "The owners will be pissed." He rose and dressed, hopping from one cold foot to the other.

"We'll figure out a way to pay them back. They have to understand if it's life

Penny of the Paranormal

or death." She pulled her hood over her head. "Ready?"

His sweet omega thought humans would have her values. Life taught him otherwise. Hopefully their team was safe where they'd left them. "Maybe we should shift to beast form. We would travel faster."

She shook her head. "We should save our strength." Her gaze avoided his. "My wolf isn't that strong. She's very flighty."

"She was strong enough to pass all those tests the vampire loves." Alistair had heard the stories from others in the pack as he had recuperated from his wound. Deathly obstacle courses and scavenger hunts. Somehow Penny had passed where others had failed.

"Only because Clare and Ian had my back. This is the first time I'm on my own."

He cupped her face with his hands. "You're not alone. I have your back too, and you're amazing."

Her shy smile melted the ice in the air. "I'm glad you think so. Still not shifting."

"Why not?" It occurred to him that he'd never seen her in wolf form.

"Because I can only shift once a day. I'm not a hunter, Alistair. I want to keep the shift for an emergency."

"Oh." He never gave the process any thought. Shifting was fast for him and he could change as often as he wanted. "Makes sense." Maybe he should start paying better attention to others around him and less on himself.

"Ready?"

He shoved his hands deep into his pockets. "Ready."

Penny opened the door and an icy blast of wind blew her hood off. "Whoa, this is going to suck."

Alistair took the lead, blocking the wind and breaking the trail in the newly fallen snow. Some places it was above his knees and to her hips. The cold crisp air was good, though. It carried scents better than during the storm and he found their team easily. The climb to the outcrop of stone was a bitch and he half-carried, half-dragged Penny through the worst of it.

She leaned against his arm and caught her breath. "Thanks, that was pretty steep. How the heck did I get down that last night?"

"You didn't." He pointed to where she had gone down an easier slope. "It was faster the way we just climbed though."

"Hey!" Parker's head popped around the side of the cliff. "They're alive!" Their little team hovered by their campfire under the overhang. Snow had piled around them, forming a natural barrier against the wind and the overhang kept in the heat. It was quite cozy.

Penny rushed to their open arms. "You're alive."

Alistair hung on the edge of the group. "I guess we won't be breaking any furniture."

Vicki hurried over and included him in the hugs. "Those rabbits saved us last night. We were so starved." But he could still hear her stomach rumble with hunger.

"If I'm lucky, maybe I'll find more today." He hugged her back until he met Penny's possessive glare.

She marched over and stepped between him and Vicki. "That's enough hugging. Let's make plans. Who wants to hit the summit and capture that damn flag?" She rubbed her hands together. Alistair wasn't sure if she was eager or just trying to keep them warm.

The team agreed with her enthusiasm and gathered what little they had for the climb. "Like yesterday, collect any wood you can carry in case another storm hits us," Penny ordered. There had been no way for them to know the forecast. The manor had no electricity so that meant no television, computers or radio.

Alistair glanced at the clear skies, doubting any snow in the near future. "We've proven ourselves strong by surviving last night. We can face another storm."

"What we should worry about are avalanches," Bobby Jo added.

Penny of the Paranormal

"Well shit, one problem at a time." Alistair clapped him on the shoulder.

"Which way should we go?" Vicki huddled close to Penny.

"Up." Alistair pointed to the summit, which was still out of sight.

"There are no trails." Nick looked less than convinced.

Alistair shrugged. "We make our own just like our ancestors." They worried too much. Just like humans. Maybe that was the point of this boot camp. To remind those shifters who'd grown too accustomed to human lifestyle what they were. His pack hadn't sent anyone here. They were still close to their wolf nature. Some might say they were too close.

Balance. That was difficult to obtain. Maybe they should have sent some shifters here after all.

The climb was as grueling as he could have imagined. They walked single file with him breaking the trail. Penny followed, her gloved hand clutching the hem of his jacket.

They climbed.

And climbed.

Until they reached a sloping rock cliff. Jagged hand and foot holds were available. Hands on hips, Alistair surveyed the obstacle. "Who is our best climber?"

"Probably you," whispered Penny.

"I should be the last to climb in case anyone falls I could catch them." Ice had formed on some of the holds. "I don't like this. We should see if there is another way around."

"No." Penny faced the team. "Anyone have climbing experience?"

Nick held up his hand. "I took it in college but it was in Arizona. Not the Arctic Circle." He approached the cliff face. "It's not a bad angle. It should be easy if it's not too icy." He started to climb. "Try to follow my steps," he called back.

Penny followed but Alistair grasped her wrist, stopping her. "Maybe you go just before me," he whispered. He couldn't protect her if they were not together.

She patted his hand. "What kind of leader would that make me?"

Penny of the Paranormal

"A safe one." He did not release his hold.

She rose on tiptoe and kissed the tip of his nose. "You'll catch me if I fall."

Her faith in him was humbling. She was right though. He'd die trying to save her.

He let her go, his heart in his throat the whole time she climbed. Finally, he followed. The ice was so cold and hard that it was easy to climb. His worries were for nothing.

At the top, he leaped over the edge, a huge grin on his face. The summit was in view.

Everyone stood ahead, their backs to him. Silence filled the air.

"What's wrong?" He pushed past them and stumbled to a halt. "Oh shit."

Alistair summed it up with those words and it broke through Penny's shock. They'd found one of the teams.

Frozen in the snow.

"Oh my God." Amy cried out and covered her face.

Penny rushed past Alistair. The frozen wolves were all huddled together against the mountainside but there had been no shelter from the storm. Snow covered most of their bodies.

She knelt next to the closest wolf and ran her hands through his snow tangled fur. "Darrell." Her voice cracked. He had once saved her from a human attack and had his arm broken. He was also one of her closest friends. She raised her gaze to Alistair. "Julia must be here too."

Panic widened his eyes.

"Dig them out." She shouted to the others. Like a whip cracking at their asses, they jumped to help.

Darrell licked her gloved hand. "He's alive!" she cried out, digging harder. "Vicki, start a fire from the wood we're carrying." She shook her friend as his eyes opened but they seemed unfocused and sluggish. "Darrell."

Alistair appeared carrying Julia's wolf form and set her next to her mate, Darrell. "They were both protecting their

Penny of the Paranormal

team from the outside edge so they got the brunt of the storm."

Penny stared at the small fire Vicki was making. It wouldn't be enough. These wolves needed more heat and shelter or they would die. On the side of this mountain, they would find neither. "We need to go back."

"But we're so close to the summit." Bobby Jo pointed to the mountaintop.

She shook her head. "We can't leave them here. There's a cabin at the bottom of the mountain where Alistair and I spent the night. There's shelter and wood for fire."

"We'll all be sent home," murmured Parker.

"I don't give a flying squirrel about winning games. These are our pack mates." She gestured to the wolves. "Everyone gets to carry one wolf down the mountains however you can."

Chapter Ten

Darrell's body weighed heavy on Alistair's shoulders. The big wolf bared his teeth once when Alistair lifted him from the ground, a flash of sharp canines, then he went limp with unconsciousness. Thankfully. There was no love lost between them but Alistair didn't want to fight him again, especially with Darrell in this semi-feral state.

Starved and frozen, with his team hurt, including his mate, Darrell's wolf was very close to the surface, if not in complete control.

Alistair grimaced as Penny struggled under Julia's dead weight. His old flame being cared for by his new one. Every man's nightmare. His and Julia's relationship didn't compare to how he felt about Penny. He'd been promised Julia at a young age—neither of them had a choice. There had been no love between them. Possession was how he'd describe how he'd felt about her. It was how his pack treated women.

Penny made him feel different. He couldn't place a word on the emotion except he wanted to be worthy of her. He didn't want to own her but wanted her to desire his company and his affection. That she would want him of her own accord.

The sweet omega's worried gaze met his. She cared so much for her pack mates that it broke his heart to see her so anxious.

Their team appeared just as apprehensive and no one questioned Penny's orders anymore. These were friends and they would save them. As it should be.

His father and alpha would have left Julia's team to die on the mountain if faced with the same challenge. *Win at all costs* was his alpha's motto.

He was wrong.

With a hand to Penny's elbow, he studied her stance. "Are you strong enough?"

Most wolves would have snapped at the suggestion of weakness but she just gave him a shy nod. "I'll have to be." Omegas had no reason for bravado. Their instincts ran differently than hunters. It was what made them so special.

Once again, they traveled single file with Alistair in the lead. They followed a different path down—a longer one, since descending the icy cliff face with a wolf on their backs was suicide.

Alistair glanced over his shoulder.

Penny remained right on his heels, a thin sheet of sweat on her forehead, even in the cold. A determined look in her eye. The cabin was still miles away but it was all downhill. Penny wouldn't give up when it concerned her pack and he feared she'd push herself too hard.

At a familiar turn in the trail, Alistair paused. "We need a break to catch our breath." What he'd do for a drink of water. He licked his chapped lips for the hundredth time.

Penny of the Paranormal

Penny sank to her knees and settled Julia next to Darrell. She stroked their fur, murmuring words of comfort.

He squatted next to her, eyeing the others who huddled on the other side of the trail. "We have a problem."

She nodded. "They'll most likely be feral when they wake up." It was good that she had noted this possibility. He wondered if the others had come to the same conclusion.

From the time they became shifters, they were taught about the dangers of hunger and stress. These were natural triggers in all creatures, including man. In shifters that meant the wolf took control. No sentience. No friendships. No pack bond. Just hunger and the pure animal instinct to survive.

"If they wake up." Alistair turned her face toward him. "I won't jeopardize your safety." He brushed his sore lips over her cracked ones and it was the sweetest of moments. His heart twisted at her touch. "I just can't."

She cupped his windblown, numb face in her gloved hands. "I'm their omega and their friend. Darrell and Julia won't hurt me, even in feral form."

He did not agree. Not with days of hunger driving these wolves. His heart knew she wouldn't abandon them to the elements, but his instinct didn't run parallel to Penny's. She was healer, mother, nurse to the pack. He was a pain in the ass, hunter, spoiled brat.

He swallowed what little was left of his pride. "What do you want to do, Omega?"

Her worried expression softened. "Their wolves will need to feel safe before relinquishing control. Shelter, warmth, and… Food." Sadness caressed her face. "Hunt for them, Alistair."

He gave her a slow blink, surprised at her request. "How?" He gestured to Darrell who he'd been carrying for over an hour. Darrell was a heavily muscled wolf who strained even Alistair's back.

She sighed. "I'm not sure, but if they wake without food, they'll definitely try to eat one of them." Her sad stare moved to their team. "I can't let that happen."

Penny of the Paranormal

Bobbi Jo rose at her comment. "She's right. I can carry two of the smaller wolves of Julia's team if someone else can manage Darrell. That wolf needs to lay off the sweets once we get home."

"If we ever get sweets again," mumbled Vicki.

"Or home," Amy added.

They were all tired and hungry, but at least his team all had a meal last night. "Enough of that kind of talk." Knowing Darrell and Julia, they probably hadn't taken the time to hunt yesterday, choosing to reach the flags over their hunger. "We'll get back." Allowing impulse to move him, he kissed Penny's forehead. "You're a wise leader. I'll do as you ask." So far, she'd kept them safe and from losing themselves to their wolves. Something Julia and Darrell hadn't accomplished. She was amazing. "Can you find the cabin from here?"

"I recognize this area from this morning." She pointed further down the hill. "Look, there's our tracks in the snow."

Alistair took in their ragged group. The wolves she'd chosen as her team—the ones he wouldn't have picked. Pride swelled his chest. They were survivors. Not the strongest of their pack, but somehow, they had managed to make it through the boot camp trials where others couldn't. Unlike him, their power and strength came from within.

"I'll be back as soon as I can find food." If he could find prey and if he could catch it. Rabbits were one thing, but in general wolves hunted in packs. Alone was hard and he hated being alone. But they needed him. This was the first time he truly felt part of the pack so technically he carried them with him. He undressed and left his clothes with Penny before shifting to beast form.

Fur coated his skin and blocked the wind. Scents grew sharper, the clear cold air made it easier to track. He rubbed against Penny as he passed.

Her gloved fingers trailed in his fur. "If you can't find anything, come back before dark."

Penny of the Paranormal

They wouldn't have that long before her pack mates warmed and woke up ravenous. If he didn't find anything in an hour, he'd be back to protect her.

The cabin finally came into view. Tears of relief burned Penny's eyes before freezing to her eyelashes. She swore she'd never live north of the frost line again. Her legs shook under every step. Julia had grown heavier as they descended the mountain.

Somehow Bobbi Jo had managed to carry two wolves while Parker struggled under Darrell's huge form. The wolf's tail and back paws actually dragged in the snow behind him.

She'd never realized how big their beast forms were in comparison to their human ones until now. Opening the door, she entered the cabin. She crossed the small room and settled Julia's slim form by the fireplace. Her friend's chest still rose under her hands but wasn't visible to the eye. If she didn't warm her pack mates soon they would slip away.

One by one, her team stumbled inside, depositing their burdens alongside Julia.

"Where's the firewood?" asked Vicki.

Penny's shoulders slumped and she pointed to the furniture. "Break them up." Somehow she'd have to figure out how to pay the cabin owners back and she hadn't a cent to her name.

Nick didn't hesitate as he smashed a chair against the floor.

She rose to her feet and closed the cabin door, watching her team create a huge fire. Her heart pounded as Darrell opened an eye, his gaze meeting hers before closing again. There had been nothing of her friend behind that look. She pressed her back to the door, gripping the doorknob behind her.

The team slowly returned to her side as the cabin warmed. Wide-eyed and shivering, they waited.

"Maybe we should…umm… Run away while we can?" Nick peeked out the window. The sun was sitting behind the trees.

Penny of the Paranormal

"They would only track us down like deer." Not to mention, Penny wouldn't leave her pack mates trapped in a cabin for Alistair to find alone. They would tear him limb from limb and she wouldn't abandon her fierce hunter. "We make a stand here."

"I searched the cupboards. There's no food." Amy took Penny by the hand.

She knew this already. Alistair and her had eaten what little they had found last night. Whoever owned this cabin hadn't planned on returning soon so it wasn't well-stocked.

"We'll wait for Alistair. He'll catch something." She had faith in him even if no one else did. He'd never been given a real chance to be the best shifter he could be until now. He hadn't let her down. She didn't expect him to.

The cabin grew warm enough that she removed her jacket and gloves. They burned the chairs and the boys were taking apart the table when Darrell lifted his shaggy head.

The room went still.

Penny stood closest to him. Her heart racing. "Darrell?" She knelt slowly, gesturing for the others behind her to move out of the cabin slowly.

The big wolf sniffed her extended hand, ears back, canines exposed.

She dropped her gaze, appearing as submissive and small as possible.

The cabin door creaked as her team hurried out into the cold. Luckily, Darrell's wolf form was still groggy and disoriented. Maybe he was still in control. She could only hope because if he was, any others in his team would follow his lead since he was so dominant, no matter their mental state.

As the last member of her team slipped out the cabin, Penny crept backwards toward the exit. Sweat trickled along her spine. She hadn't really thought this plan out. She had hoped Alistair would be here when the other wolves woke but Darrell had warmed quickly.

The big wolf nuzzled his mate until she stirred. The commotion had the other wolves waking as well.

Penny of the Paranormal

As Penny moved closer to the open door, Darrell swung around with a snarl.

An involuntary squeak of surprise escaped her and she scrambled for an escape.

Darrell leapt across the room with paranormal speed and was met by a larger golden wolf midair.

Alistair!

Penny was pressed flat as he crushed her against the wall. Growls echoed in the small space and she couldn't see what was transpiring. Click of claws on wood, followed by hungry snarls outside.

Was Alistair letting them escape the cabin to attack her team? She beat her fist against Darrell's back.

After what felt like an eternity, Alistair moved, allowing her to rise to her feet. She expected to have to fight for her life.

Instead, she watched Julia's team feast on a freshly killed doe.

Penny hugged Alistair around his thick furry throat. "You did it."

CHAPTER ELEVEN

After the other team had finished eating the doe Alistair had caught, they shifted back to human form. Everyone now gathered around the dying fire inside the cabin. One of Darrell's teammates borrowed some clothes found in the cabin and went with Nick to retrieve the other team's belongings left at the base of the mountain.

Penny sat between Alistair and Darrell, separating them, with Julia on the other side of her mate. Their gazes landed everywhere but on each other. To say things were awkward was an understatement. Naked pack mates, ex-fiancée, and going feral made for uncomfortable conversation.

Alistair had his arm over his omega's shoulders and her pack mates tossed him unsure glances. Darrell's were clearly disapproving. Alistair didn't care. All

Penny of the Paranormal

that mattered was how Penny felt about him.

Thankfully, Nick and the other shifter returned quickly with everyone's clothing. Nudity wasn't what made him uncomfortable. He didn't want anyone freezing and wasn't used to feeling all this…empathy.

"What now?" Penny rested her head on Alistair's chest.

"We should go for the flags." He stroked her hair. They had been so close to the summit. It would be a shame to give up now.

"Why do you care?" Julia snapped. "Why are you even participating and don't give me this bullshit story about wanting Pallas's car. I know you, Alistair. You could buy five of those cars and not put a dent in your bank account."

Darrell's eyes went round. "He could? Really?"

Alistair's traitorous gaze darted to Penny.

"Really?" Julia echoed her mate, her expression just as stunned as his.

"What?" Penny looked from him to Julia and back again. "Ian asked him to even out the teams to make it fair. You heard him, Julia. Now leave Alistair alone." She set a possessive hand over his thundering heart.

Not that he needed protecting from others but it was sweet that Penny felt the need to defend his honor. He kissed the top of her head. "I don't want anyone from my team to be sent home. I think we should have time to reach the summit and return to the manor if we leave now."

"I don't want to go home," said Vicki.

"Nobody wants to go home." Darrell rested his arms on his knees as he stared at the small flames.

"We're out of fuel for the fire." Alistair gestured to the bare cabin. "No matter what, it's going to be a cold night. Better to keep moving."

"Easy for you to say. Your team didn't almost die on the mountainside." Julia hugged Darrell's arm.

Penny of the Paranormal

"Not true." He rested his chin on Penny's head, needing her close as he recalled how near she'd come to freezing to death.

"I hate to admit this, but I agree with Alistair," Darrell finally spoke. "We can't give up. We have to keep pushing."

Penny gave Alistair a wink and mouthed the words. "Good job."

His heart could have burst at such outward approval. "Grab what blankets and clothes you can find so we can stay warm in case we get caught in another storm." Alistair helped Penny to her feet and with her jacket. "This will be harder to do at night. You need to stay close to me at all times." He couldn't bear to lose her. Not again.

She nodded. "We can do this."

Except for finding the frozen team, they would have accomplished this goal already and been returning to the manor by now.

"Let's go," Darrell called out and exited the cabin.

Alistair bristled at the command but his omega ran her hands over his tense shoulders, calming his dominant wolf. This wasn't his pack, no matter how much he wished. He had no right to lead them or make trouble. Darrel was their most dominant hunter and the teams should follow him. He, at least, took Alistair's suggestions with more grace than Alistair would have when he first arrived to the boot camp. The man he'd once been seemed like such a stranger now.

Both teams shuffled out into the snow. The weather on the summit would be worse. He watched the tired steps of the other shifters, none of whom asked to quit and return to the manor.

As if sensing his thoughts, Penny leaned closer and whispered, "Some of us don't have the option to fail."

"What you mean?"

"Their packs won't accept them back if they fail the boot camp. For some, this is home."

Alistair fisted his hands. That explained why many of the shifters were so driven. "Then they're outcasts if we fail?" He knew exactly how that felt.

"Ian will take them into his pack, but as long as he's training at the boot camp he can't care for those who have no home. Pallas owns the manor, not us. The outcasts have to wait until Ian and Clare graduate." She wiped her red nose. "I know that sounds heartless, but—"

"No." He shook his head. "I think it's honorable that Ian is offering them a home." Most wouldn't have. Outcasts didn't tend to get a second chance. When he returned to his pack without Julia, he was sure to be cast out. The thought didn't cause knots in his guts like it had a few days ago. He caressed Penny's face. Maybe not returning home wouldn't be so bad. Maybe leaving his pack might actually be a good thing.

The last of the shifters left the cabin so Alistair and Penny followed them out. He shut the door with a silent promise to right the damage they had done to this place.

They hiked along the mountain. The moon hung low in the sky, silhouetting the stark bare branches of the trees as the wind howled down the mountainside.

Wait. Alistair stopped. "Quiet everyone." He waved his hands at the other shifters. He twisted around, scanning the forest, and listened closer. More distant howling. Not the wind.

Darrell paled and gripped Julia's hand. "You don't think?"

"I do." Ian and Clare's team were out there and in wolf form, howling as if on a hunt. Drawing closer. As they had just recently witnessed, hungry, cold shifters could go feral fast. Not recognizing friend from foe, pack from prey.

"Shift," Alistair ordered Penny.

Without question, she unzipped her jacket with shaky hands.

"Shift," he commanded their team. Julia's people were too exhausted to change again so soon. "We need to be prepared to defend the other team." He met Darrell's worried stare. "Keep your people together while we ring you."

They were exposed in the forest. "Which way to do you want to run? Cabin or manor?"

"Manor. It has more defenses," Darrell replied. "They'll tear into the cabin easily."

Alistair stripped and started his own shift. They could fight better this way with tooth and claw as weapons. It was possible Clare's team was tracking game, but he had hunted this mountain. Prey was sparse. He'd been lucky to track a sick doe.

The only trail this side of the peak were theirs.

Julia gathered her team in a tight bunch and Penny's team circled them.

She stood at his side, pale fur gleaming in the moonlight. Her delicate little paws danced in the snow as adrenaline pumped into her bloodstream as it did in his.

Even though tiny for a wolf, she remained steady at the front, ready to protect her pack.

Those who thought omegas were weak, were wrong. They were the heart. She would fight just like any shifter, but her drives were different than a hunter's.

A huge wolf broke through the line of trees in the distance. He ran straight for them, not pausing or slowing. Teeth bared.

"Shit." Darrell pulled Julia behind him. "They *have* gone feral."

Someone screamed.

Alistair twisted in time to see the rest of Clare's team break from cover around them. She'd chosen the strongest and fastest of the pack. Each wolf outweighing their team members easily.

They didn't have a fighting chance.

Darrell must have had the same thought since he shouted, "Run!"

Heart in throat, Alistair shoved Penny toward Darrell's group, then rushed toward the Ian's growing form. He was their only chance of stopping the alpha from killing his own pack. He couldn't let Ian harm them. If he did, they'd never trust him again. From what he knew of Ian, he was a good leader. Someone Alistair could look up to and aspire to be.

The scramble of claws at his side caught Alistair's attention. He tossed a look over his shoulder, expecting to find a feral wolf ready to attack. Instead, he found Penny, struggling to match his pace.

Ian's huge form crashed into his before he could react to his delicate omega's insane move. The alpha was a little bigger than Alistair and much, much hungrier. Sharp teeth snapped at Alistair's face as he held the alpha back with just his paws. He'd never been prey before and he didn't like it.

The alpha yelped in surprise and was suddenly off of Alistair.

Penny danced around her alpha and under him. Her small form easily moving between his limbs as she nipped at his paws until he tripped and fell. Then she was racing off after the others, not going for the kill Alistair's hunter instincts screamed for.

He shook his head, clearing his wolfish desires. Killing was not what he wanted to do. Hell, he didn't even want to replace Ian as alpha. In all truth, he didn't know what he wanted. He hadn't been given a chance to find out except he knew from now on Penny would be part of his life.

In a few long strides, he joined Penny in a race for their lives. The others ran ahead of them in human form with their team busy keeping Clare's at bay.

They were in luck. Clare's team seemed exhausted, otherwise they would have overtaken them easily. They still managed to get a few bites on Penny's team's hides.

Ahead, the manor's huge stone building came into view, the moonlight paving their path. Candlelight lit some of the lower level windows as if welcoming them home.

Ian's howl cut through the night like a knife and pumped fuel into everyone's legs. Amazing how fast they suddenly could run with the right motivation. Not long ago a hike had seemed impossible.

The sound of heavy footfalls followed Alistair across the deep snow. He could hear Ian panting as he closed the distance between them.

Unable to resist, Alistair tossed a glance over his shoulder.

Penny of the Paranormal

Clare, the alpha female, had joined her mate on Alistair's tail.

They had spotted him as the biggest threat to their hunt. He had restrained his instinct to kill Ian. That decision was going to literally bite him in the ass.

His legs crumpled as one of them landed on his back. Teeth snapped around his throat, crushing his windpipe. Clawed paws filled his vision as his face was pushed into the deep snow. He couldn't tell who was suffocating the life from him. It didn't matter. Dead was dead.

He couldn't breathe. His limbs scrabbled, pushing uselessly at the snow. He'd failed Penny. They would catch her and tear her to pieces.

Someone yelped. Was it him? Couldn't be—he couldn't even draw breath.

The paws at his muzzle were replaced by black military boots and the pressure on Alistair's throat was gone. He filled his burning lungs and coughed as his windpipe re-expanded.

Pallas's ugly face filled his vision. "That a boy." He patted Alistair's head like a pet dog. "You'll be fine."

Chapter Twelve

A high-pitched whistle split the air and had the entire racing pack twisting to a halt.

Clare's team crumpled mid-step and lay in the snow as if someone had flipped a switch off in their brains. Penny rushed to the closest wolf and sniffed. It still breathed and seemed…asleep.

From the dark emerged Pallas, Ian's great, unconscious wolf form hung easily over his shoulder and Alistair was at his side. Her hunter's throat was stained red with blood.

Her heart skipped a beat and she ran to his side and licked his neck to assess the extent of the wound.

Alistair stilled, lifting his chin so she could have easier access to the thick furry throat. His trust in her was warming. They weren't even from the same pack yet he'd bare his weakest point without question to her sharp teeth.

No pulsing blood or deep gaps in his hide. She released a breath that she'd been holding. It was not a mortal wound. He'd been lucky or some part of Ian had been able to restrain his wolf enough not to kill her hunter. Either way, her relief weakened her knees.

Alistair nudged her muzzle with his own before doing his own assessment of her for injuries. She bumped his shoulder to let them know she was fine.

She finally turned her attention to Pallas's retreating back as he approached Julia's team, surrounded by unconscious wolves. Where had the vampire come from? The manor was in view in front of them. It had been their destination, but he'd seemed to arrive from behind their trail.

Oh, who cared? She was so tired and sore and everyone lived. Let the vampire be mysterious and weird. She trotted after him. They were finally safe and she had more pressing questions to ask him.

Like could she keep Alistair?

Ian and Clare had the power to deny anyone membership in their pack, but she doubted they would refuse her choice of mate. She wouldn't ever ask anything of them but this. Pallas was the real problem. He owned the boot camp and the manor they lived in. This place was his territory. He owed her nothing and he wasn't exactly empathetic, especially when it came to matters of the heart.

Pallas gestured to the fallen wolves. "Carry them to the manor," he ordered without pausing to check if they were well. Julia and Darrell exchanged glances, then organized their team to do as ordered. The vampire marched home as if nothing unusual had happened.

A low growl rolled in Penny's chest. They had almost died. How dare he act as if it didn't matter? She ran ahead of Pallas and was surprised to find piles of clothes folded on the back porch of the manor, leading to the kitchen. She hesitated on the porch, front foot up, and sniffed. They belonged to the pack. She glanced over her shoulder at the growing figure of Pallas with Ian still slung over his shoulder. She found her garments among the folded piles and shifted to human form.

The vampire must have done this. There was no other explanation. He'd been expecting them. All this time she thought he'd been sitting by the fire, reading a book or whatever he did for relaxation. But it seemed like he'd been watching for their return.

She hated changing shape. Being in her wolf form was fine, nothing spectacular in her opinion. At least, not for the amount of suffering she had to endure to be her wolf. It was the pain she dreaded. All shifters had to deal with the discomfort, including her, but if she didn't *have* to shift then she wouldn't. Claws retracted into nail beds, leaving her fingertips burning. Joints popped and fur retreated, but the worst was the tail shrinking back into her spine. Her lower back ached awfully as she pulled on her jeans. With her tongue, she poked at her sore gums.

Penny of the Paranormal

Pallas reached the bottom step of the porch, but was no longer carrying her alpha. "Penny." He nodded. "Good to see you survived. Did your team retrieve their flag?"

She crossed her arms and blocked his path. "Are you kidding? We almost died in that storm and all you care about are the flags?"

He twisted and counted heads as the others passed them on the stairs, shifting and dressing. Alistair now stood at her back like a huge, protective shadow, his presence giving her more confidence.

The vampire looked confused. "Seems like everyone lived unless I counted wrong." He quirked an eyebrow in her direction.

"No one died," she shouted. "Would you be happier if someone had?"

He frowned. "I would be happier if someone gave me a flag from the mountain peak." He climbed onto the porch and held out his hand but no one came forward. "Nobody? Three teams and no one reached the top?"

Alistair set his hand on her shoulder as if ready to hold her back if she attacked. She'd never be that stupid. Pallas would break her with a flick of his finger. "The storm was brutal. We're flesh and blood creatures that can still freeze to death no matter what you believe."

"But you didn't." Pallas's gaze tracked over Penny's pack. "There's food in the fridge again. Go eat." He stepped aside before being trampled and glanced aside at her. "Not eating?"

"I'm too angry."

Sliding his hand under her elbow, Pallas guided her inside. "Alistair, can you bring the half cow I have stored in the freezer out to the barn where the sleeping shifters are being held? Ian and Clare will be waking soon and I don't want another attempted massacre."

"What did you do to them?" her hunter asked.

The vampire tapped his head. "Jedi mind trick."

Penny snorted. He hadn't been among them very long but was definitely

Penny of the Paranormal

adapting to their lingo. "You used your mind to make them sleep?"

"You can do that?" Alistair fell behind as he came to a stop. "My old pack associates with a lot of vampires. I have never heard of this ability."

Pallas gave him a mysterious smile. "My clan is different."

"How?" Alistair asked, his expression mystified and somewhat alarmed.

"We're the first." Pallas waved his hand, shooing Alistair to finish his task.

Penny did notice how Alistair had said his *old* pack. This loosened a knot in her gut. It sounded like he had subconsciously decided not to return to them.

The vampire guided her to his office in the basement and sat at his desk. "You don't approve of this mission."

"Of course not."

"You've never objected before and those tasks were just as dangerous."

She paced the length of his office. "We all failed this one."

"No one failed."

She twisted in her tracks. "Nobody reached the flags." If they had all passed, then they all could remain at the boot camp. Nobody would be sent home. Including her.

"Retrieving the flags was an objective but not the true mission." He steepled his fingers, elbows resting on the arms of his chair. "I had to push you to your limits. You specifically."

She sank into the closest seat, which was an uncomfortable metal folding chair. "Me?"

He leaned forward. "Did you lead your team as I instructed?"

She nodded, unable to speak.

"Alistair didn't take command?"

"He tried." She cleared her throat. "I didn't let him."

"Did you like leading?" He raised a nonexistent eyebrow.

"No, I hated it but I knew you picked me as a team leader for a reason." She had listened to her inner voice and ignored her omega instincts for once.

"But you still did it and the others followed you, right? No one else tried to take over?"

"They followed me." She still wasn't sure where this conversation was going.

"Do you want to be an alpha one day?" He leaned back into his chair and it creaked under his solid weight.

"Never." That would be against her nature. "I don't like leading." She enjoyed caring for her pack mates, not making decisions for them.

"Do you care where in the pack hierarchy you stand?"

"I'm omega." She shrugged. "I'm at the bottom."

"That's what makes omegas special." He grinned as if what he said was clear as mud.

She waited for him to continue explaining what he thought was obvious, but he was oblivious. "I don't understand."

His smile faded. "Omegas are the heart of the pack, Penny. That's a really important role and it seems like one you've been ignoring. When someone is acting out of turn, like your alpha, they need to depend on someone, whose mind is clear of dominance, to speak out. Someone they can trust with the pack's well-being."

She rubbed her temples, a headache starting behind her eyes. "Alphas don't listen to omegas."

"Good alphas do. Ian and Clare will. It looks like Alistair will as well. You needed to find your voice and learn to speak out. Every pack needs at least one omega to keep them sane. The voice of reason that isn't blinded by dominance lust. When an omega speaks out for the pack, a good alpha will listen." Pallas sighed, a distant look in his eyes. "I wonder if that's what has gone wrong with modern packs. So many things have changed." He blinked as if coming awake and shifted his weight in the chair. "My elite team will need an omega."

"I'm the only omega at the boot camp."

"So I had to make sure you are the best."

Penny of the Paranormal

"Are you telling me this whole exercise was to teach me to stand up for myself and for the pack?" Nausea made her gut heavy. He had almost killed everyone. Most of the pack had gone feral. If it hadn't been for Alistair, her team would have done the same.

She felt the blood drain from her face. Julia's team would have frozen to death and everyone else feral to do damage to anyone who crossed their paths until they were well fed. The small town of Alberg was only a few miles away. What if they had wandered into it as a feral pack?

"You risked a lot of people's lives. You're a monster." The accusation was out of her mouth before she could filter her words.

His fangs glinted in the artificial light as he grinned. "Remember this exercise and how close you came to losing your pack the next time you feel too meek to act."

She sat stunned as things fell into place in her mind. All those terrible things could have happened but they hadn't because of the little decisions she'd made following her omega heart. She wanted to vomit but there was nothing in her stomach. This was a lesson she'd never forget. Nor would she ever forgive Pallas for delivering it. The burden of such responsibility weighed heavily on her slight shoulders, but for her pack, she'd bear it.

Pallas tilted his head as if listening. "Come in," he called out before anyone knocked. She hadn't heard any footsteps so whoever was outside the office could move quietly when they wanted.

The door swung open and Alistair entered with two plates stacked high with sandwiches, cheese, and grapes. He set one in front of her. "You need to eat."

She didn't want food, but her wolf did. Unfortunately, the vampire had annihilated her appetite so she nibbled at some cheese.

Alistair pulled a chair next to hers and met the vampire's obvious dislike of being interrupted. "Don't mind me." He shoved half a sandwich in his mouth and chewed.

How did he manage that without choking?

Rolling his eyes, Pallas watched her hunter for a moment longer. "I was explaining to Penny that she won the mission."

Alistair swallowed his mouthful with effort. "But nobody retrieved their flags."

"The true goal was to keep your team from going feral." He turned his icy gaze on Penny. "I never doubted you. Did you doubt yourself?"

She set her cheese aside, her upset stomach worse. Last thing she wanted was to toss her cookies in front of these two men. "Of course I did. I don't understand how you could believe that I could keep my team safe. Hello, look at me." She had no misconception of herself. Her one true strength was being able to see through bullshit and that included her own.

"What are your thoughts on Penny's performance, Alistair?" asked Pallas.

"I think Penny should eat more. She's been through a lot." Her hunter picked a grape from his plate and fed it to her. "I will admit to having doubts about her team reaching the flag. As to keeping her team from going feral? I wasn't concerned. She had it under control."

She swallowed the grape that tasted like saw dust. "You believed in me." That was the best thing anyone had ever told her.

"You're omega. You place the needs of the pack first." His gaze softened at her clear confusion. "Look, the first thing you ordered me to do was hunt for your team. You could have ordered me to go for the flag by myself instead. You made sure they were fed, warm, and safe. Those were your priorities. If the other two teams had you, they never would have gone feral."

"Exactly." Pallas clapped once. He gave Alistair an appraising look. "You explained that well. Look what happened to the other teams. They came unglued without an omega."

Penny of the Paranormal

"But during the other exercises, there was only one omega. That didn't make a difference."

"The other missions weren't as grueling, but I will point out that those who worked with you always came ahead, achieving their goals."

"Oh…" Her heart suddenly felt lighter than it had in years and her chest swelled with—with what must be pride. "I did do a good job." She grabbed Alistair's hand. "With some help."

He kissed her knuckles. "It was all you, babe. I was just muscle."

Pallas's gaze narrowed at the small exchange. "Can there not be a mission without copulating?"

Heat seared across Penny's cheeks but Alistair's grip on her hand didn't lessen.

"Where's the fun in that?" her hunter asked. He kissed her hand again. "Speaking of fun, what did you do to my car?"

Pallas's eyes widened. "Your car is still parked outside."

"Not the Porsche. The car I won in our bet. By your own admission, Penny achieved your goal and by default so does my team, and none of them quit." Alistair bit into another sandwich, this bite much more manageable so she didn't have to worry about the Heimlich.

"No flag, no deal." Pallas's tone was glacier. She could see frost forming on the walls.

"It's a draw," she shouted. The last thing she wanted with her taskmaster killing her new lover over a stupid car. "No car, no personal slave for a year."

"The car is totaled anyway. Didn't you just get it back from the garage?" It was like Alistair had a death wish. He just kept poking at the angry vampire waiting for him to sting.

She shoved the other half of Alistair's sandwich in his mouth. "You'll need your strength for tonight." She answered his shocked expression.

He grinned around his sandwich, the shock melting to something more heated. He chewed with more vigor. She hadn't

Penny of the Paranormal

meant it that way, but okay. She wasn't opposed to the idea either.

Pallas made a disgusted noise. "I crashed the car in the snow storm and I don't want to hear anything about karma."

She hid her smirk behind a bite of her own sandwich, her appetite finally resurrecting.

"As the winner, Penny, what would you choose as your prize?" The vampire leaned back.

"I get a prize?"

"Since neither I or Alistair got one, somebody should. I'm pleased with you and feeling generous. It won't last so pick quickly."

She gave Alistair a side look.

"No." Pallas shook his head.

"Yes," she shot back.

"No," he repeated.

"It's my choice. It's my prize."

"I don't want pets in my boot camp."

She ran her fingers through Alistair's hair. "He's not a pet, but he's mine."

Alistair's chewing slowed, his stare moving from her to Pallas then back again.

She fiddled with a few strands of his hair, unable to meet the vampire's glare. If Pallas denied her, how could she stay if her heart was thrown out? She didn't want to leave the boot camp, but she would if it meant staying with Alistair.

Pallas dropped his head into his hands. "I can't believe you just thought that. This is why I'm not a generous person. Every time I try to be nice, I end up adopting another wolf." He waved his hand for them to leave. "Go and take him with you. Make sure he follows the boot camp rules, but he bunks with the boys, not you."

She jumped to her feet and raced around the desk to kiss Pallas on his bald head. "Thank you." She then grabbed Alistair by the hand and led her confused hunter out of the basement.

CHAPTER THIRTEEN

Penny and Alistair bypassed the kitchen filled with hungry shifters snarfing down sandwiches. She gave a deliberate quiet exhale as she spotted Ian with Clare on his lap, both laughing at something Darrell said. No hard feelings about going feral seemed apparent. Pallas had stopped them in time.

She paused on the stairs and glanced at Alistair. "I thought they were locked in the barn."

He shrugged. "When I arrived with the meat, they were already shifting back to human form. Whatever Pallas did snapped them out of being feral. Thought they'd rather eat with everyone else than raw beef, naked in the barn."

She kissed his cheek.

Amusement danced in his eyes. He appeared younger and happier than she'd ever seen him. "It was Ian who pointed out Pallas's smashed car hidden in the barn. If the alpha had been so hungry and anxious to get to the kitchen, I think he would have cried."

"He can mourn the silly car later." She brought Alistair to the bedroom she shared with Clare. Technically, the alpha female didn't sleep there anymore. She kept her clothes stored in the bureaus since the small room she used with Ian didn't have space for furniture besides their bed. Penny had offered to switch rooms, but they seemed happy in their cozy space up in the attic with no neighbors.

Pallas didn't like fraternization within the pack while training but it was happening whether he liked it or not. For a vampire, he was a bit of a stick in the mud when it came to shifters and sex.

Alistair closed the door behind him as she set their plates on a small beside table by her bed.

"I wanted a moment alone with you while I still have the courage to ask you something." She tugged on the hem of her sweater and licked her lips. Silly

Penny of the Paranormal

how nervous she suddenly was. She wanted him to remain at the boot camp and had spent a lot of time with Alistair over the last few days. He never had anything good to say about his pack so why were there butterflies making her stomach sick?

"Does this something have to do with my being your pet?" He chuckled as a blush painted her face.

"That's not what I meant. I mean—that's what Pallas said, not me. What—what I want—want…" She scraped her fingers through her knotted hair and her throat grew so tight she could barely breathe. Her heart raced.

Alistair would never say yes. The other night in the cabin had been a way for them to stay warm. Yes, he had said some sweet things but it had been a spur of the moment that inspired those words, not his heart. Why would a hunter like him want to stay in a broken down manor with no electricity?

"Shh." He collected her in his arms, rested her head on his chest and stroked her hair. "I was just kidding. My feelings

Annie Nicholas

weren't hurt. I'd be happy to be your pet."

"You would be?" To her horror, she hiccupped. She had eaten her sandwich too fast.

His gaze grew half-lidded and warm. "As long as I can lick you."

Her face burned again and she pressed it deeper in his sweater. Though he did have a magical tongue.

"What were you going to ask me, Penny? I'm dying to know." He lifted her chin so their gazes could meet.

"I want you to stay." She swallowed the lump in her throat. "Will you stay, here, at the boot camp, with me?" That was a lot to ask a shifter. To not return to his pack for a girl he'd only just met. Alistair had more to lose than the average shifter. His family had money and power. He could be their next alpha if he wanted. He just needed a mate worthy of that challenge, but she couldn't be that person. She had no taste to rule over others.

He'd been a serious jerk when he arrived at the boot camp but he had

Penny of the Paranormal

changed. Being separated from his toxic pack had helped. She didn't want Alistair to change back to a jerk. She loved him just the way he was.

Penny brushed her fingertips over his full lips and recalled how they felt against hers. She didn't want him to leave because she'd miss his overbearing protectiveness, his sharp sense of humor, his courage. She never thought she would meet a hunter who made her feel so confident. Most men took from her. They took her affection, her help, her energy, leaving her an empty, lonely shell. How could she ever fall in love with anyone if all they did was leave her tired?

Alistair did the opposite. He bolstered her. Filled with emotions and joy. Without him, she would survive, but life wasn't about just surviving. She wanted to *live* and he made her life happy.

His face was serious. "I never planned on leaving. I don't care if Pallas gave me permission to stay or not. You complete me." He lifted her in his arms so their lips met. He kissed her long and deep, massaging the back of her neck as he sat on the edge of her bed.

She brushed her tongue against his in a tease of her own. A growl sounded in his throat as she pressed forward, crawling onto his lap. This felt like home. Right here, straddling his hips as his hands ran over her back and gripped her tighter. Nothing she felt had ever come close to being with him.

When her breasts heaved, they brushed his chest, sending currents of desire straight to her core. He sucked on her bottom lip and rattled a hungry sound, drawing a gasp from her.

She rolled her hips against the thick erection that pressed against his pants. He gripped her hair, angling her neck so he could trace her throat with delicate kisses. Shivers of anticipation ran down her spine. She couldn't believe he was going to stay for her. Her heart felt ready to explode from joy.

His hand slid under her shirt, up her ribs, and unsnapped her bra with flick of his fingers. He cupped her breast and she arched against his hand. His touch set all her never endings tingling. He pulled her sweater over her head, tossed it to the floor, and pressed his mouth to her breast, lapping at the sensitive bud. Pulling away, he blew air until her nipple drew up tight and she just about came undone. The man was a beast and she liked him like that.

Desperate for more, she guided his hand to the button of her jeans.

Plucking gently at her breast, he pulled her nipple into his mouth and grazed his teeth against it. The button of her jeans came undone under Alistair's attention and her zipper followed. He slid his hand under her panties and cupped her wet sex. He smiled, sexy and slow. "You know how to make me feel welcome." He slid his finger into her slick entrance and brushed her clit with his thumb. It drove her mad with want.

She bucked helplessly against his hand. "Oh!" she cried out.

"Fuck, you're so beautiful." He pulled his finger out slowly, then added a second as he pressed into her. She quivered with desire. Leaning forward, he nipped her bottom lip and matched her pace with his hand.

She was so close to finishing. He brought out such strong emotions in her. Things a shifter should feel, even omegas. Right when she was about to cross over the edge, he went still. She tangled her fingers in his hair, pressing her forehead to his so their gazes were locked. "You're mine."

"I am. Forever and ever."

With a steadying breath, she lifted off his hand and shimmied out of her jeans. "I want all of you." She loved how his gaze caressed her curves as if he'd never seen another so alluring.

In one smooth motion, he rose to his feet and pulled off his sweaters while she worked on his jeans. He eased his thick cock from his briefs and stroked his length.

Her heart drummed against her chest. He was very ready for her.

He paced forward with a predator's grace. "I like how you look at me."

Penny of the Paranormal

"How's that?" She barely managed those words, the English language fading from her mind.

"Like I'm a chocolate sundae you're ready to devour."

She grinned and sensed her wolf rising. He knew her so well. He'd backed her to bed, easing her onto the mattress and spreading her legs. Dragging his tongue along her slick seam, he moaned. She gasped with the pleasure that blasted through her body. She closed her eyes as his rough cheek scrapped across her inner thigh. His tongue lapped at her with long, languid strokes.

Then he crawled over her body, placing tender kisses along her bare stomach. "You're mine as well, Penny."

She dragged her fingernails over his shoulder and sighed as happiness filled her. "Always."

He growled low and plunged into her, stretching her core. He felt so good. His lips collided with hers and she witnessed his eyes change to his wolf. Hers reacted in kind. The shift small yet potent.

She bowed against him, nails clawing his back. She wanted him to mark him, for him to feel her, here and now. This wasn't just fucking—this was more. She felt it in her bones.

He bucked hard, pulling her tight against him. His teeth grazed her throat.

She shouted his name, not caring if the whole manor heard her climax.

He arched back, muscle taut, tendons standing out in his neck as he came. Hot jets filled her. He plunged into her a few more times as his cock emptied. Spent, he nuzzled her collarbone and stroked her thigh. "I love you Penny." He said it so softly she almost missed it.

She smiled at the ceiling and ran her fingers over his ribs, her heart full of hope for the future. "I love you too."

CHAPTER FOURTEEN

"Come on, you punch harder than that, Nick." Alistair circled Nick in the challenge ring.

Penny smiled to herself as she sat on a snow bank just beyond the ring. Her hunter was helping Pallas teach hand-to-hand combat to those who wished more training, like Nick and Parker.

Nick lashed out at Alistair, fists a blur with his shifter speed yet her hunter dodged every attempt to strike him.

"Good." Alistair clapped the smaller werewolf on the back. "Let's take five." Heat steamed off his bare chest as he strolled toward her. The cold air making it visible. His shoulders rolled with his predatory grace. With a tub of popcorn, she could watch move all day. "Hey gorgeous." His smiled widened as he spotted her.

Annie Nicholas

She pouted as he pulled a sweater over his head. Oh well, she didn't want him to freeze either. "Hey, yourself."

"What do you have there?" He pointed to a basket at her feet.

"A little surprise."

He paused, tilting his head. "Is this the kind of surprise Pallas would spring on me?"

"No, never. This is a good thing." She patted the snow next to her.

He plopped down, swinging his arm around her shoulders.

"The people who own the cabin accepted your offer." She handed him a set of keys. "You are now the proud owner of a partially destroyed hunting cabin."

He threw back his head and laughed. "So what's the basket for?"

"Picnic lunch. I thought we could spend the night and figure out what needs to be repaired in your new home."

He leaned forward, kissing the tip of her nose. "Our new home and for anyone else who needs one until Ian and Clare

Penny of the Paranormal

can find one for them. No homeless wolves. No outcasts."

She'd hoped he would say that and threw her arms around his neck.

Thank you for taking the time to read Penny of the Paranormal. If you enjoyed it, please consider telling your friends or posting a short review. Word of mouth is an author's best friend and much appreciated. Next book in the series, Pallas, is now available for Pre-Order! Stay up to date with my new releases, giveaways, and news by joining my newsletter. As a thank you, a link to a free novel, Ravenous, will be sent to you via email.

Annie Nicholas

Pallas

Vanguard Elite, book 5
Releasing April 17, 2017

I came from the deadliest vampire clan that ever existed.
Spent centuries transforming wolf shifters into warriors.
People trembled at my name.
Now, I run a boot camp for misfit werewolves.
Everything is coming together. My life, the pack, and our community.
Then they found a corpse on my land.
Drained of blood.
My only hope of proving my innocence is the sheriff.
The woman of my dreams with a warrior's heart.
But she hates me.
For now.

Penny of the Paranormal

Annie Nicholas

Not His Dragon

Eoin Grant hasn't encountered a female of his race in decades, and this crazy person's scent declares her unmated. Fate set her in his path, and he won't let this opportunity slip through his claws. No matter how wary she is of him. After all, how many chances does a dragon have at finding love? But fate can be a crueler mistress than his perfect mate. Of all things, she thinks she's human.

Business is taking off for Angie Weldon. She put her freakishly sharp nails to good use when she opened her back-scratching spa in downtown New Porter City. The local shifter community pounced on her skills and she's knee-deep in shed fur. By the end of the year,

Penny of the Paranormal

if lucky, she could afford to move out of her crappy apartment.

Dollar signs flash before Angie's eyes when a dark, brooding stranger books her solid for a week but she notices the possessive fury in his glare. She's been around enough shifters to know the look, and she won't go down that road again. Angie is literally swept off her feet by the intense shifter and he wants more from her than she's willing to give. She figures it's best to avoid eye contact and back away slowly. Until he changes her life by insisting she's a dragon.

Annie Nicholas

THE OMEGAS

Only a vampire is man enough to teach werewolves how to fight.

Pretty librarian Sugar wants her life to stay quiet. That's hard enough when friends and neighbors turn into furry werewolves every full moon. But when a hot vampire gets involved, life's bound to get complicated.

The Omegas have always been the pansies of the paranormal. Now Chicago's top werewolf pack has issued them a life or death challenge. Their only option: hire a vampire warrior to teach them the moves.

Daedalus has been a powerful vampire for ages. Intrigued by the chance to train the geeks of the underworld, he wasn't bargaining on losing his heart to a human. Can he make the Omegas a success, fit into Sugar's quiet life, and avoid being ripped to shreds in the process?

Books by Annie Nicholas

Vanguard Elite
Bootcamp of Misfit Wolves
A Taste of Shifter Geekdom
Blind Wolf Bluff
Penny of the Paranormal

The Vanguards series
The Omegas
The Alpha
The Beta
Omegas in Love
Sigma
Prima

The Angler series
Bait (Free)
Catch
Hunting Colby
Release

Chronicles of Eorthe
Scent of Salvation

Scent of Valor
Scent of a Scandal

Lake City Series
Ravenous (Free)
Starved for Love
Sinful Cravings

Stand Alone Books
Not His Dragon
Irresistible
Koishi
No Refuge
Boarded

For more information on coming releases go to
http://www.annienicholas.com

ABOUT THE AUTHOR

Annie Nicholas writes paranormal romance with a twist. She has courted vampires, hunted with shifters, and slain a dragon's ego all with the might of her pen. Riding the wind of her imagination, she travels beyond the restraints of reality and shares them with anyone wanting to read her stories. Mother, daughter, and wife are some of the other hats she wears while hiking through the hills and dales of her adopted state of Vermont.

Annie writes for Samhain Publishing, Carina Press, and Lyrical Press.

www.annienicholas.com
Facebook
Twitter
Annie's Newsletter

Annie Nicholas

Published 2017
Copyright by Annie Nicholas
Cover design by J. Hemmington

All rights reserved. No part of this publication may be reproduced, stored in a retrieval system, or transmitted in any form or by any means, electronic, mechanical, recording or otherwise—except in the case of brief quotations embodied in critical articles or reviews--without the prior written permission of the author.

This is a work of fiction. The characters, incidents and dialogues in this book are of the author's imagination and are not to be construed as real. Any resemblance to actual events or persons, living or dead, is completely coincidental and not intended by the author.

Manufactured in the United States of America

I love hearing feedback. Email: annienicholas@ymail.com

Printed in Great Britain
by Amazon